Mountain Dog Rescue

A STORY OF A
BERNESE MOUNTAIN DOG

Look for these books
in the Dog Tales series:

One Golden Year

The Westie Winter

Mountain Dog Rescue

The Great Spaniel Escape

DOG TALES #3

Mountain Dog Rescue

A STORY OF A
BERNESE MOUNTAIN DOG

BY COLEEN HUBBARD

Illustrations by Lori Savastano

**AN
APPLE
PAPERBACK**

SCHOLASTIC
New York   Toronto   London   Auckland   Sydney
Mexico City   New Delhi   Hong Kong

For Allie, Natalie, and Willa —
my daughters and dog lovers.

ISBN 0-590-18977-8

12 11 10 9 8 7 6 5 4 3 2 1   9/9 0 1 2 3 4/0

Printed in the U.S.A.   40
First Scholastic printing, January 1999

CONTENTS

ONE

Inventors at Work

"Hey, Dad!" shouted Jon Ziller. "Catch!"

A fat snowball exploded on the shoulder of Al Ziller's flannel shirt as he emerged from his wood-working shop. The shop was just a few long strides away from the log home where the Ziller family lived in Peak, Colorado.

"Gotcha!" Jon laughed. "I finally gotcha!"

"I wasn't ready!" Al joked. "I saw you get off the school bus from my window, and the next thing I know, you're ambushing me!" He brushed the soft snow from his shirt and ran his hands through his short, graying blond hair. He was tall and athletic-looking, just like Jon's older brother, Eric.

Jon knew he looked more like his mother — a

· 1

little bit skinny, with dark wavy hair, and a smile that turned up higher on the left side. He didn't mind looking like his mom, but he desperately wanted to grow tall and strong like his fourteen-year-old brother.

"You always duck too fast, Dad," Jon explained. "Ambush is the only way to get a guy like you!"

Al watched as his son, using a long-handled plastic contraption, quickly formed a half dozen new balls from the snow covering the ground outside the shop.

"What in the world is that?" Al asked, walking over to investigate.

"This," explained Jon with pride, "is my latest invention. I call it the Super Snowballer. I put the finishing touches on it at school today."

"How'd you make it?" Al asked, a hint of amazement in his voice.

"Well," said Jon, "I used two plastic ice cream scoops, two yardsticks, a simple spring, and some strapping tape."

"You're too smart for a ten-year-old," Al said, shaking his head in admiration. "How do you think of things like this?"

"It's not the *how* that's important, Dad. It's the *why*."

"What do you mean, son?"

"Every great inventor comes up with an idea because he or she sees a need for something," Jon answered.

"And you saw a need for a Super Snowballer?"

"Exactly!" said Jon. "Because with this invention, I can make snowballs twice as fast and not freeze my hands. And then I might stand a chance when Eric and his friends ambush *me*!"

"I see," Al replied. "May I try it out?"

"Sure," Jon answered. "The spring's not quite tight enough, but go ahead."

Just as Al was getting the hang of the Super Snowballer, Jon's dog, Mogul, came bounding out of the shop. Mogul was a large, three-year-old Bernese Mountain Dog. He ran directly for Jon and nearly knocked him down in excitement.

"Hey, Mogul!" Jon called happily. "Hey, boy! What'cha been doing? Sleeping the day away under Dad's workbench? You ready to play now?"

Jon, like all dog lovers, thought *his* dog was the best dog in the whole world. As far as he was concerned, there wasn't a handsomer, gentler, more devoted, and funnier dog on the planet! And anyone who hadn't experienced the pleasure of meeting a Berner (as they're often called) didn't know what they were missing!

Mogul, who was three years old, was Jon's first and only dog. The Zillers had had him since he was a somewhat wild but adorable puppy, given to them by a college friend of Al's who bred Berners on his farm in eastern Colorado. Jon's mother called Mogul the "Gentle Giant" and said that his personality was a perfect fit for their family. Jon decided the first moment he set eyes on Mogul that he would always have a Bernese Mountain Dog for his pet — no other dog would do!

Jon watched as Mogul frolicked in the snow, releasing only a fraction of his boundless canine energy. The dog ran in fast, joyful circles around Jon and his dad, dipping his nose in and out of the powdery snow. Then he stopped, flopped on his back with all four feet in the air, and wriggled vigorously while snow flew up around him.

"He goes crazy every afternoon when you come home," Al observed with a chuckle. "How do you explain that? All morning he naps in the shop while I work — and then the minute you arrive he springs into action."

Jon chased Mogul between two tall pine trees, then back to where his dad stood watching. "He just likes me," Jon said, leaning down to pet the panting dog on his soft black head. "And I trained him. We understand each other. Don't we, Mogul?"

Mogul looked up at Jon with his gentle dark eyes and cocked his head to the side. His black tail wagged furiously, showing how happy he was.

"Well," said Al, stretching, "I should get back to work. I have a headboard to finish. What are your plans this afternoon?"

Jon ruffled the fur on Mogul's neck, making the dog's tags jingle in the quiet air. "Rosie's coming over so we can work on our entry for the January Invention Convention at school."

Rosie Johnson was Jon's fourth-grade classmate and good friend. She lived just down the road from the Zillers, so her house, too, was outside of town and away from the busy ski resort that made Peak famous. Rosie and Jon shared a passion for inventing and were always partners for the annual invention competition at Peak Elementary. Just the year before they had won second place for their battery-operated soup stirrer!

Best of all, Rosie wasn't nuts about skiing. And in a town like Peak, that was a rare thing. Both Jon and Rosie preferred snowshoeing and sledding to fighting the crowds on the busy slopes of Peak Mountain.

"I'll be in the shop if you need me," Al told Jon. "Mom's working late, so I'll make some spaghetti for dinner after a while."

Jon watched as his dad returned to the shop,

closing the wooden door behind him. Within minutes, Jon heard the high, steady hum of the electric
sander. He could picture his dad bent over the
wood, safety glasses on his face, concentrating as
he put the finishing touches on a beautiful oak
headboard.

Al Ziller's handmade furniture could be bought
only in the finest boutiques along the main street
of Peak. Jon knew that families from France,
Switzerland, and Mexico bought tables and chairs
and beds made by his father's careful hands.

I wonder, thought Jon, *if anyone will ever buy
my inventions? Will anyone ever think I'm as talented as Dad or Eric?*

Mogul barked, trying to get Jon's attention,
and Jon returned his focus to the wriggling dog.
Mogul had the classic coloring of all full-breed
Berners — a beautiful combination of black,
white, and tan. His head and body were glossy
black, with a white blaze marking his forehead
and muzzle. His chest bore a cross of white fur,
and the end of his wavy black tail and tips of his

paws were also white. And to add further interest, Mogul had matching tan eyebrows, tan cheeks, and tan markings on his four strong legs.

"You're a handsome dog, aren't you?" Jon said. "And a big one!" Mogul weighed at least a hundred pounds, though he was surprisingly agile for his size. Though he was fully grown now, Jon could still remember Mogul as a tiny puppy. His markings were the same, only in miniature, and his coat was so soft and fluffy that people had always wanted to hold him like a little baby. But even then, Mogul preferred to be active and would squirm away to explore and play.

"You're an athlete like Eric, right, boy?"

To prove his point, Mogul bounded toward the trees again, kicking up snow and weaving between the closely spaced evergreens. Jon knew that Mogul was never so happy as when he was running and playing outside. Berners needed plenty of space to exercise.

Then Mogul began barking and running for the road. Jon chased after him, guessing that the dog had spotted Rosie. Sure enough, there was his friend, dressed in her red parka, heading up the steep road that led to the Zillers' driveway. Jon ran down to meet her, waving his mittened hand.

"Hey, Rosie!"

"Hey, Jon!"

Jon watched as Rosie bent down to greet Mogul with a kiss on the head. They were great friends, even though Rosie was more of a cat person — she and her two older sisters had two fat yellow cats who slept on the windowsills of their bedrooms.

Jon thought Rosie was very pretty, even though they were just good friends. She usually wore her light brown hair pulled back from her face with a colored headband — she had lots of different colors — and her skin was shiny and pink. She had a gap between her two front teeth that Rosie's mom said would disappear once she had braces, but Jon thought it was kind of cute. When she smiled, she had matching dimples, which looked like fingerprints in soft dough.

But the best thing about Rosie, thought Jon, *is that she laughs all the time. She doesn't get too serious about things, the way I do.*

As the two friends walked slowly back toward Jon's house, they discussed ideas for new inventions. Rosie thought they should invent something that would make all the tourists in Peak suddenly disappear.

"Think about it," she said. "The ski slopes would be empty, the restaurants would be empty, the shops would be empty!"

"But that wouldn't be good for your parents," Jon reminded her. (They owned a restaurant right in the middle of town.)

"True," sighed Rosie. "We get tired of all the tourists, but that's how we survive, right?"

"Right," Jon agreed. "If Peak weren't a glitzy ski resort, our families wouldn't have jobs. The tourists buy my dad's furniture, eat at your parents' café, and stay at the tourist hotel where my mom works."

"Okay," Rosie said with a laugh. "The tourists

can stay. We can always look forward to April when they go home."

Just then Mogul stopped in his tracks and shook his body furiously. Snow and mud flew everywhere, spraying Jon and Rosie.

"Yuck! At least cats don't do that!" Rosie wiped a blob of mud from her jeans.

"You should see how mad my mom gets when Mogul does that inside," Jon said, rolling his eyes. Then his whole face lit up with interest. "Hey — what if we invent a special pet mat that gets all the snow and mud off of a dog?"

"What do you mean?"

"Well, something that's better and easier than just using an old towel. Dogs never want to stand still to be dried off."

"You always want to do dog inventions," Rosie complained. "Remember the glow-in-the-dark pet leashes and the water bowl that wouldn't freeze over?"

"Those were great!" Jon protested. "Besides,

I'm thinking of our future. Pets are big business. We have to think about a future market for our inventions."

"I'll think about it," Rosie said. "Fact is, I don't really have a better idea. But — "

"I know," Jon interrupted. "You're a cat person."

"I can't help it. But I do like *your* dog."

"That's because Mogul's the best dog in the whole world."

Rosie laughed and leaned down to pet Mogul. "So, tell me more about this pet mat."

As Jon explained the seed of his idea, he watched his house come into view. No matter how many times a day he saw this same sight, it always gave him a warm feeling. He liked the way his two-story log house looked against the snowy mountains. He liked the curl of smoke coming from the brick chimney and the large, shiny glass windows that looked out at the valley below. He liked knowing that his father had designed and built the house himself, twenty years before when

Peak was still a sleepy mountain town with some great local skiing.

Jon especially loved the fact that his parents had been married in that very house, and that he and Eric had lived their entire lives in such a cozy, peaceful place.

"Don't you wonder how people can stand living in the city?" Jon mused, interrupting his own explanation.

"They probably wonder how we can stand living in the mountains. We don't have malls or big movie theaters, and our school is so small that all the teachers knew us when we were babies, and are best friends with our parents!"

"That's what I love about it," said Jon. "I love everything about Peak — except the tourists. And sometimes the ski thing drives me crazy!"

"True," said Rosie. "You and I are among the intelligent few who prefer not putting skinny boards on our feet and falling down a mountain."

"I love the outdoors. But skiing is sort of — boring."

"I know. Pretty weird, when your brother is the big ski champion of the whole town."

Jon nodded his head. It *was* weird, because unlike Jon, Eric lived to ski. He was a truly gifted cross-country racer. And now that he was in high school and skiing with the local club, he placed first in more and more racing events. The shelf in his bedroom was beginning to groan under the weight of all his trophies. And his name was in the *Peak Daily* almost every other day.

"Do you think he'll go to the Olympics?" Rosie asked.

"He wants to. But there are a lot of steps between here and there. I don't really understand all the levels of competition. We're going to Breckenridge for a big race tomorrow morning."

"Cool," said Rosie. "I have to help Mom and Dad clear tables at the café. Saturday is a big breakfast day. I'll be covered in syrup and orange juice by ten A.M."

"But they pay you," Jon reminded her. "You have the biggest bank account of anyone I know."

"I'm saving for college," said Rosie. "I'm going to make sure I go to the best engineering college in the country. Even if it takes a lot of Saturday mornings stacking pancake plates!"

Rosie laughed her famous laugh. Jon knew that Rosie managed to have fun even while clearing plates at her parents' café. She *always* seemed to have a great time.

Just then, a four-wheel-drive car with peeling black paint chugged past them on the dirt road. The horn blared, making Mogul jump and head for the ditch.

"It's your brother and his prehistoric friends," said Rosie, rolling her eyes.

"His ski team buddies," said Jon. "They'll be in the kitchen when we get there, eating everything in sight. Then they'll go down to the basement and lift weights and get all sweaty."

"Yuck," said Rosie. "But you know what's worse?"

"What?"

"The guy driving the car is dating Polly." Polly

was Rosie's oldest sister, who went to high school with Eric.

"Double yuck!" groaned Jon.

"I know. He does dishes at the café on the weekends. He and Polly flirt all day long."

"Gross!" yelled Jon. "Don't tell me any more about it! Hey, I have an idea!"

"What?"

"Let's go make a huge pile of snowballs with my Super Snowballer. Then I'll call Eric and his friends outside and we'll ambush them!"

"Great!" shouted Rosie. "Let's go! I'll beat you there!"

Rosie and Jon took off running up the driveway. First Jon was ahead, and then Rosie.

But the clear winner was Mogul, who beat them both by a mile.

TWO

Eric Wins Again

"Wake up, Jon," whispered Bonnie Ziller, leaning over her son's rumpled bed. "It's time to get up." She laughed to herself as she noticed an opened book about famous inventors spread across the foot of his bed.

"What time is it?" Jon mumbled. He was still in the clutches of deep, winter sleep. It was dark outside, and all he wanted to do was burrow under his down-filled quilt and stay there for hours.

"It's six-thirty. We have to get ready for Eric's race."

Bonnie sat down on the edge of the oak bed, which had been designed and made by her husband. The headboard had cutouts of an owl and a wolf, two of Jon's favorite wild creatures. Jon opened one eye and smiled at his mom. She was already dressed in jeans and a warm wool sweater, her long dark hair pulled back into a simple pony-tail.

When she worked at the front desk of the Peak Alpine Inn, she always wore her hair swept up in a complicated twist with pretty clips and pins. And she wore fancy black suits with scarves in bright colors. But today, she was dressed comfortably and casually, and Jon thought she looked especially pretty.

"Do I have to go, Mom?" Jon already knew the answer, but he figured it was worth a try.

"Of course you have to go. We would never leave you alone all day."

"But I wouldn't be alone," he offered. "Mogul would be with me."

Bonnie laughed and reached over to turn on the bedside lamp. It cast a faint glow in the dark room. "Some baby-sitter Mogul would be! Can he make you lunch? Can he handle an emergency? Can he dial nine-one-one?"

"No," Jon agreed, "but he would keep me entertained. Besides, I'm working on a new pet invention, and I need Mogul to be my model."

"You can work on that tomorrow," said Bonnie lightly. "Today we're going to watch Eric ski at Breckenridge. It's an important race."

"Why?" Jon asked, yawning wide. It seemed to him that all of Eric's races were important. Important enough for the whole family to get up early almost every Saturday during ski season and drive all over the Rocky Mountains.

"If he does well today, he qualifies for a bigger race next month. And that one qualifies him for — "

"I know," Jon interrupted. "An even *bigger* race."

"Right. We need to give him the old family support."

Jon was silent for a minute. Eric always got the old family support. In fact, he got the support of the entire town of Peak. Everyone was always talking about what a great skier he was, and how he would probably qualify for the Olympic Cross-Country Team someday, after winning a scholarship to race on an important college ski team.

"Okay," Jon sighed. "I'm getting up. Just give me a few minutes."

"Is anything wrong? You seem a little grumpy."

"Mom?" Jon asked, swallowing hard.

"Yes?"

"Do you and Dad — do you guys think I'm, well, talented at anything?"

"Of course we do!" Bonnie responded, sounding surprised. "We think you're a really talented inventor. You have an amazing mind for science and technology!"

"But that's not as good as being an athlete, Mom."

"It's not better or worse. It's just a different talent. Like people always say, you can't compare apples and oranges."

"Or watermelons and grapes." Jon tried hard to keep his voice from cracking.

Bonnie took Jon's hand in hers and squeezed it

with emotion. "Jon, you know Dad and I think *both* of our sons are talented and special. We're crazy about both of you! It's just that Eric's skiing is more visible right now."

"Especially to Dad."

Bonnie looked down into Jon's brown eyes and shook her head. "That's not true, Jon. It's just that Dad was once a competitive skier, too — "

"Until he wrecked his knee."

"Right. Anyway, he likes following Eric's progress. But he's proud of you, too. And you'll have your turn in the spotlight, I promise!"

"Thanks, Mom." Jon appreciated his mother's attempt to make him feel better. But it didn't help much. Right then, he just felt like the invisible younger brother, who would be ten and skinny forever.

But before he could think any more about it, Mogul came running into Jon's room, bumping into the desk and then the side of the bed.

"Hey, boy!" Jon cried. "How're you doing?"

Mogul sat down on the rug, waiting for the af-

fection he knew would eventually come his way. Sure enough, Jon propped himself on his side so he could stroke his dog's soft fur and silky ears.

"Mogul loves you better than anybody else," Bonnie commented. "Just look at how he watches you!"

Jon smiled. He was secretly glad that his mom recognized that to Mogul, at least, Jon was top dog — no pun intended. Even though Mogul loved all the Zillers, it was clear that Jon was his favorite human.

"That's because I trained him," Jon explained. "And I have time to spend with him. When you and Dad are working and Eric is practicing, Mogul and I hang out together."

"It's more than that," observed Bonnie. "You have a special way of communicating with each other. It's really neat to watch."

"Did you hear that, Mogul? Mom likes you! I told you she likes you! Mogul's afraid you don't like him because he sheds so much and knocks things over inside the house."

"Well," Bonnie said with a laugh, "I admit that I'd be very happy if you could invent something to keep him from shedding. But I think he's a terrific dog, anyway."

"He can't help it, Mom. Shedding is just a natural trait of Berners, right, Mogul?"

Mogul turned his head to look at Bonnie with pleading eyes. Then he gave her a lick on the back of her hand.

"He's saying thank you," Jon explained.

"Tell him he's welcome. Now, you need to get up and get ready. Okay?"

"Okay." Jon watched his mom leave the room. Then he turned to Mogul. "I wish I could stay home with you and nap all day. But I have to go watch Eric win his fifty-millionth trophy. I'll play with you later this afternoon."

Mogul gazed steadily at Jon, as though he understood completely.

Sure enough, Eric did win another trophy. He took second place in his age category, which was good enough to qualify him for the next big race.

On the way home, Eric and Al discussed the possibility of Eric going to upstate New York for an important race several months away. Bonnie slept, her head against the window, and Jon gazed out at the snowy landscape.

"Are you drinking enough?" Al asked Eric, looking at him in the rearview mirror. "I don't want you to get dehydrated."

"I won't." Eric took another gulp of neon-green sports drink from the huge plastic bottle that seemed to be permanently glued to his hand.

Jon thought Eric's sports drinks tasted like a horrible mixture of fruit punch and crushed-up multivitamins. He didn't know how Eric could stand to drink them — but there was a lot about Eric's life that Jon didn't understand.

For instance, Jon couldn't figure out how Eric could enjoy doing the same things in the same order every time he raced. Each race day, the Zillers had to arrive at least an hour and a half before the race. Eric would then stand in line for his race bib with the big black number, which he wore over his jacket for the judges to see. Next he had to carefully choose the appropriate wax for the snow conditions and spend a long time waxing the bottom of his skis.

After waxing and checking his equipment, Eric would warm up his muscles with stretches and bends. Then he always took off for a short ski, testing the wax and the snow. Finally, he had to eat a high-energy snack, gulp some more sports drink, and line up at the start with dozens of other skiers.

During all of this, Jon and Eric's dad played the role of coach and manager — holding things for Eric, bringing him food, giving him tips and encouragement, and always, always filling up the silly water bottle with green glop! Only when the race was about to begin did Al join Bonnie and Jon at the sidelines. There he would pace impatiently back and forth until the gunshot sounded to signal the start of the competition.

It was always the same, Jon thought. Even the postrace events were predictable. While everyone waited for the awards ceremony, Al helped Eric put on a dry shirt, eat more, drink more, and stow his equipment. And predictably, Eric would step up to the platform to accept a first- or second-place ribbon, medal, or trophy. Then Jon and his parents would hug Eric, shake his hand, pat him on the back and say, "Way to go! Great race! Congratulations!"

The sameness of the sport was what Jon didn't understand. There were no surprises — and being surprised was what he loved most about inventing. You could start with one thing in mind, and then it would change entirely by the time you were finished! You never knew exactly how a project would turn out.

And at that very moment, as the car zoomed along the highway toward Peak, Jon was busy thinking about his pet mat invention.

As though reading his thoughts, Al looked back at Jon in the rearview mirror and smiled. "You thinking about your invention?"

"Yeah," Jon sighed. "It's complicated."

"Why?"

"Well, Rosie and I want to make a pet mat that will absorb mud, slush, and water from a dog's feet. But it has to be washable, and it has to be portable — I can't figure it all out yet."

"I know that feeling," Al replied. "Sometimes when I design a new piece of furniture, it seems impossible to get it all right — the kind of wood, the perfect mix of beauty and function — it's overwhelming."

Jon smiled to himself, happy to know that he and his dad shared the same feelings about their work. In fact, creating a piece of furniture out of wood and making an invention out of odd materials were actually very similar. More similar than woodworking and skiing! But just as he was about to ask his dad a question, Eric changed the subject — back to himself.

"So, Dad, you think I should try for the race in New York? Would you be able to come with me? What would we do about a sponsor?"

Jon looked out the window again, realizing that

for the rest of the way home, Eric and Al would discuss nothing but cross-country skiing.

Jon reached into his backpack for a sketch pad and pencil. He began to make a few quick drawings of what he was now calling the Wet Pet Splat Mat. He tuned out the sounds of his brother and dad talking about skiing and focused his own busy thoughts.

Jon could hardly wait to get home and try out some of his new ideas. He couldn't wait to hear Rosie's ideas.

And he knew Mogul would be a patient and willing model, as usual. Mogul was always the very first dog to try each of Jon and Rosie's pet inventions.

I'm on my way home, Mogul! thought Jon.

THREE

The Worst Day Ever

"Aren't you taking the bus home?" Rosie asked Jon after school on Monday.

"I'm walking over to the hotel to hang out with my mom. My dad had to drive down to Denver for a shipment of wood, and Eric has ski practice."

"Oh," Rosie sighed. "I was hoping we could work on our invention. We only have a few weeks left before the competition. And we have to submit a rough plan by Friday."

"I know," Jon responded. "I'm trying not to panic."

Rosie laughed her famous laugh and threw her backpack over her shoulder. "Don't worry, we'll be fine. Can we get together tomorrow?"

"Sure!" agreed Jon. "Come to my house so we can try things out with Mogul."

"Okay. Say hi to your mom!" Rosie climbed aboard the long yellow bus and took a seat near the back.

Jon waved at Rosie until the bus was out of sight. Then he ambled down a small hill toward the main street of Peak, called Peak Avenue by tourists and simply The Ave by town residents. Even though the weekend was over, groups of skiers crowded the sidewalk, peering into shop windows or sitting on benches in the bright winter sunshine. Everyone seemed to be sipping coffee or licking ice-cream cones. And everyone had the relaxed smile that comes from being on vacation in a pretty resort town.

Six blocks later, Jon reached the Peak Alpine Inn and pushed through the heavy glass revolving door. He spotted his mom behind the front desk, talking to a man and woman. Jon knew he shouldn't disturb her, so he took a seat in the plush, quiet lobby, watching people come and go in shiny snowsuits and heavy ski boots. A fire blazed in the enormous stone fireplace, and a man in a black tuxedo played soft tunes on a grand piano in the corner of the room.

Finally, the couple left the desk and Bonnie motioned for Jon to come over. She gave him a quick hug and opened a small door that led to the back office of the hotel.

"Make yourself comfortable, honey," she said. "I got you some cookies and milk from the kitchen. Do you have homework?"

"A little math, and I need to work on my invention. May I use the computer?"

"Sure," Bonnie responded. "I need to go back to the desk. Dad should be here pretty soon to pick you up. Call me if you need anything."

Jon hung his coat on the back of a chair and settled down in front of the computer. He took a diskette out of his backpack and scanned through his notes for the Wet Pet Splat Mat. He and Rosie were pretty sure of their materials now, but not of the actual construction. So far, they knew they needed suction cups, sponges, rubber sheeting, adhesive, wood, and some plastic. But how would it all go together? Jon couldn't wait to begin building, and experimenting with Mogul.

A half hour later, Jon realized he was starving. He stood up, stretched, and looked around for the cookies his mom had mentioned. He found them, nicely arranged on a white china plate on his mom's desk in the corner. Beside them stood a tall glass of milk. Jon sat down in the swivel desk chair and happily munched a chewy peanut butter cookie.

On the wall above his mom's desk, Jon noticed at least a dozen newspaper articles about Eric and his ski races. Eric's face beamed in the yellowing photographs, and his arms were full of medals and trophies. The words "fantastic" and "incredible" and "unbelievable strength and speed" seemed to jump out of the newsprint before Jon's eyes.

What would that feel like? Jon wondered. *To have those words written about yourself? Fantastic! Incredible!*

Suddenly Jon felt very lonely in the empty office. He wished Rosie were there, or even better — Mogul! It made him laugh to think of Mogul tearing around the fancy hotel, knocking over vases of flowers and crashing into statues and fountains. But at that very moment, Mogul was probably chasing around his large, fenced dog run, waiting for Jon to come home and play catch.

Just then, Jon heard the office door open. He spun around in the desk chair to see who it was, and his elbow sent the glass of milk flying. He tried to catch it, but it was too late.

Oh, no! he thought as the milk made a river of white all over a pile of folders on the desk.

"No!" he heard his mother cry out. She hurried over and snatched up the folders before they were completely soaked. Jon grabbed a box of tissues and tried unsuccessfully to mop up the spill.

"I'm sorry, Mom. My elbow knocked it."

"I know. It was an accident." But Bonnie's voice sounded tense and worried. She tried shaking the folders and liquid sprayed over her desk. A few drops hit the newspaper clippings on the wall, leaving small dark stains.

"Were they important papers? I'm really sorry."

Bonnie tried to smile, but her lips were tight. "They're informational packets about Peak, to send to guests. I spent all morning putting them together."

"Can I help you fix them?" Jon asked hopefully. "I could make new packets."

"Thanks," Bonnie said, patting Jon on the shoulder. "But you know what? I'll have to make new copies of everything. And I can't let you play around on the copy machine."

"I wouldn't *play*," Jon protested. "I just want to help."

"I know. I just meant — I'll have to do it later. Don't worry, Jon. It's not such a big deal."

"Okay." Jon threw a soggy pile of tissues into the trash can and gave his mom a hug. She hugged him back hard, but Jon still felt bad.

I'm so clumsy! he thought. *Mogul and I —*

we're always knocking things over! We're not graceful like Eric.

"I came back to tell you that Dad's here to pick you up," Bonnie remembered. "Are you ready to go home?"

"Yes," Jon said quietly. "I need to give Mogul some exercise."

"Well, I'll see you when I get home. And don't worry about the milk."

Al laughed when Jon told him the story of the spilled milk. But he wasn't laughing later when Jon had his second accident of the day — in his father's shop!

After Jon and Mogul had played in the snow until both were sweaty and tired, Jon went over to the shop to hang out with his dad. Mogul followed happily, glad for a chance to rest. The dog headed immediately to his favorite place — the narrow space underneath Al's desk.

Jon loved everything about his dad's work

space — the smell of cut wood, the sight of the tools hanging in orderly rows on the wall, the sounds of jazz playing on the small radio. And he loved to watch Al work. He admired the expert way his father measured and cut, sanded and polished. His father could make the challenging work of building furniture look like an easy, effortless thing to do.

"You picked up a lot of new wood," Jon commented. Stacks of long boards filled the back half of the shop.

"I have a big order to fill!" Al looked happy as he described the six desks he would be building for a real estate office in town.

"They're going to be Mission style," he said, pointing to a picture in a book.

Jon looked over his father's shoulder at the photo.

"See how beautiful the design is, Jon? No fuss, no frills!"

Jon turned the slick pages of the book, studying photographs of tables and chairs and beds and desks. He was happy about his dad's new project. He was proud that his dad made such useful and handsome things. And he wished with all his heart that someday *he* would be able to make useful things, too. Things that people needed and wanted — things that made their lives easier.

"Can I help?" Sometimes Al let Jon work beside him, teaching patiently as they went along. Jon had learned lots about basic construction over the years — knowledge he often relied on in putting together his own inventions.

"Sure," said Al. "Let's see." He looked around and spotted a partly finished dresser in the corner. "You could help me drill the holes in the drawers where the knobs will go."

"Great!" said Jon. He loved to drill. He'd learned how to do it several years ago, and he was proud that he could handle a drill safely and with a fair amount of precision.

"Use this template to mark where the holes go," Al said, handing Jon a thin piece of wood, almost like a ruler, with premarked holes. "Right in

the center — six inches across and three inches
down. Be sure to clamp down the template, and
make your marks with this pencil."

"I know, Dad," Jon responded, somewhat impatiently. This was easy. He'd marked drill holes
dozens of times before.

"Okay," said Al. "Go ahead. I need to return a
few phone calls."

Al sat at his small, cluttered desk beneath the
window, causing Mogul to scramble out of his favorite place and wander over to Jon.

"Sit!" Jon told him, and Mogul obeyed. "I need
to concentrate, so you just sit still."

Mogul stared up at Jon patiently, obviously
hoping that Jon would change his mind and pet
him or play with him. His tail flipped back and
forth, batting the legs of the workbench and the
backs of Jon's knees.

"Stay!" Jon cautioned Mogul. He clamped the
template on the first piece of wood and made his
light pencil marking. *Perfect!* he thought. *Easy
enough!*

He reached for the drill, carefully positioning the sharp bit over the place he had marked. He guided the drill with steady pressure, watching as it pierced the wood and created a snug hole where the knob would go.

Then he began the process again, clamping the template and making his soft pencil mark on the second drawer. Mogul, who was growing impatient for attention, slapped his tail harder and gave Jon a playful nudge with his muzzle.

"No, Mogul," Jon said, moving his leg out of range. "Not right now — I'm busy."

Jon turned the drill on again, concentrating on his aim and the proper angle of the tool. Just as the metal bit made contact with the wood, Mogul jumped up and rested his two front paws on the workbench. The dog's sudden movement startled Jon, causing the drill to slip.

"No!" Jon shouted as the drill tore a jagged hole in the wood. "Down, Mogul! Down!"

Mogul slunk away, his nose near the ground and his tail no longer wagging.

"What happened?" Al said, hurrying to Jon's side.

"Mogul bumped me and made my hand slip!"

Al examined the damage, shaking his head.

"It's ruined, isn't it?" Jon asked.

"Yes. I'm afraid so."

"I'm sorry, Dad. I really am. I was being so careful."

"Sounds as if it was Mogul's fault," Al sighed.

"No," said Jon. "It's my fault. He was in his dog run all day while we were gone, and I guess I didn't give him enough time to run around when I got home."

"I thought you had him pretty well trained. I heard you tell him to sit."

Jon looked over at Mogul, who was standing by the door, waiting to be released. "He usually obeys really well. I think he's just hyper today."

"That happens, I guess." Al took the drawer front and placed it on top of a scrap pile. He didn't sound mad, but Jon knew that he wasn't exactly happy, either. His simple mistake with the drill would cost his father more time, and more money in wood.

For the second time that day, Jon felt truly awful. *I keep messing up! First with Mom and now with Dad. Eric never makes mistakes, and I can't seem to stop making them.*

"Don't worry about it," Al said, coming over to give Jon a hug. "I mess up all the time. I think you're just having one of those days."

Jon sighed. "I think I'll go watch TV. That way I can't ruin anything."

"Just don't blow it up," Al joked, trying to cheer his son.

But Jon didn't feel like joking.

He called Mogul to come with him and left the shop. Mogul followed happily, panting with excitement just to be with Jon.

"You're the only one who doesn't think I'm clumsy," Jon told his dog as they walked back to the house. "I don't know what I'd do if I didn't have you."

FOUR

All the Great Inventors

"Hey, Mogul," said Jon, "hold still!"

But Mogul didn't want to stand still. And he especially didn't want to stand still inside a wooden box, even though the top was open and there was a door. The dog turned in circles, trying to find a way out.

"Just for a few more seconds!" Jon pleaded. "I just need to see if the sides of this box are tall enough!"

Mogul sat down, giving Jon an especially indulgent look. He seemed to be saying, "Okay, fine. I don't know what this is all about, but for you I'll sit still."

"Thanks, buddy." Jon smiled, reaching over the two-foot-high hinged door to pet Mogul's head.

"I'm almost done, and then we'll go outside and play!"

Mogul gave a throaty bark upon hearing the words *outside* and *play*. He lived for his romps in the snow with Jon. But Jon was determined to get some work done on the invention first, because the Invention Convention at school was just over a week away.

So far, Jon and Rosie had figured out that the Wet Pet Splat Mat had to have sides at least two feet high in order to catch the moisture that an average dog would vigorously shake from its fur. And the design was going pretty well. They were both pleased with their idea to line the entire box with linoleum, and to cover the bottom of the box with a removable sponge pad that could be washed and used over and over.

Rosie had come up with the idea of putting large suction cups on the bottom of the box, so that it wouldn't slide back and forth when a dog was inside. But Jon worried that the entire box was too heavy and awkward, and that it was too big for the place where most people would want it: by their back door.

"That's the thing about inventions," Jon said to Mogul, letting the dog out of the box. "It can take a long time to get one right, and Rosie and I don't have a lot of time left."

Mogul licked Jon's face and slapped his tail against the box. He wanted to play, and he clearly didn't care in the least about the complicated problems that inventors had to deal with.

"See, Mogul," Jon continued, "all the great inventors have faced the same challenges. Getting the idea for an invention is just the beginning. Then you have to design and experiment and sometimes start all over again. It's a long process. I mean, look how long it took Henry Ford to make a mass-produced car affordable for the average American family."

Mogul yawned and sat down, still looking hopefully at Jon.

"But the thing that keeps you going is knowing that you have a chance of changing history! Not just keeping dogs from dragging mud and water inside, but changing history!"

By now, Mogul had given up. He lay on the kitchen floor, then rolled over on his back, all four feet in the air. Jon got the message and stroked the white patch of fur on Mogul's chest. Mogul sighed with pleasure, content to be petted if he wasn't going to go outside after all.

"Look at the Wright brothers," continued Jon. "They changed history when their airplane finally worked in nineteen-oh-three. Then there was the invention of the telescope way back in sixteen-oh-eight. And television in nineteen twenty-six. And the laser in nineteen sixty. And how about computers and space shuttles! Not that the Wet Pet is going to change the course of history, but it's a start!"

Jon's voice had risen to an excited pitch, so he didn't hear the front door open. The next thing he knew, Eric and two of his friends were standing in the kitchen, laughing hysterically — at him.

"Hey," said Eric, "are you talking to yourself, Jon-O?"

"No!" Jon looked up anxiously at the three big guys with their puffy down coats and bulging gym bags. "I was talking to Mogul."

This made the guys laugh even harder. Mogul stood up protectively and leaned against Jon.

"Your brother is nuts!" Eric's friend Drake said. "Do your parents know he talks to himself?"

"They're used to it," Eric said. "He's the original nutty professor."

"And what's with the box?" asked the other friend — a tall guy named Ronny who had a nearly shaved head and a small gold earring in his left ear.

"It's — it's my invention for school," Jon stuttered. He wished they would just go down to the basement and leave him alone. He hated it when he felt stupid and young around Eric and his friends. He wished he could disappear! He wished his dad would walk in from the shop and talk to Eric about ski practice.

"What's it for?" asked Drake, pretending to be interested in the wooden box. But Jon knew that whatever he said would be turned into a big joke by the older boys.

"It's to dry off your dog when he comes into the house," Jon said softly, "so he doesn't get everything all wet and muddy."

"Hey, can I try it out?" Ronny teased. He jumped inside the box and stamped around. He pretended to shake like a dog, making dumb growling sounds and barking noises. This made Eric and Drake nearly fall over with laughter. They sputtered and coughed and held their sides as if it were the funniest thing they had ever seen.

Mogul looked a little anxious. He cocked his head toward Jon, who was turning red in the face.

"Don't!" Jon cried. "Leave it alone!"

"We're just joking around," Eric said. "Chill out!"

"You're going to break it!" Jon insisted. "It's not even finished! Why don't you just go lift your stupid weights and leave me alone!" Jon was so mad and embarrassed he felt like crying. But there was no way he would ever let these goons see him that upset.

"Sorry," Ronny said, stepping out of the box. "No harm intended, kid. We're just playing around."

"Yeah," Eric added. "We're just goofing on you." He put a brotherly arm around Jon's shoulders and pounded him on the back. The pounding hurt a little, but Jon stood still and made himself look tough. "You're a great kid. And we're going to let you get back to your invention, okay?"

You just don't want me to tell Mom, Jon thought. *You don't want to get in trouble and risk not being allowed to go to one of your races!*

"Right," Jon said, looking down at Mogul. It was clear that Mogul didn't particularly like Eric's friends. The dog had positioned himself solidly between Jon and the older boys. Jon knew that dogs had the ability to sense conflict among humans, and Mogul was reacting to the obvious tension in the air. When strangers came into the

Ziller household, Mogul tended to stick close to family members until he knew that everything would be fine. Loyalty was a wonderful trait in all Berners.

"See you," Drake and Ronny called out, pushing past Jon and heading for the basement steps. "Good luck, Einstein!"

"I'll bring some food down," Eric called after them. He grabbed a bag of cookies and a bunch of bananas and followed his friends.

After they were gone, Jon carried his invention up to his bedroom for safekeeping. He didn't want Eric and his friends messing around with it just to be funny. Mogul followed Jon upstairs and then back downstairs to the front door.

"Let's go outside," Jon said, putting on his coat.

Mogul stood at the door, panting. He was so excited he couldn't stop wiggling.

The minute he was free, Mogul ran straight up the hill behind the Ziller house. Then he ran back to Jon's side, urging him to come along. But Jon had spotted Rosie coming up the driveway.

"Hey!" he called to her. "I didn't know you were coming over!"

"I didn't, either," Rosie smiled. "But I finished my homework, and my mom said I could come over until dinner to work on the invention."

"Great!" Jon tried to sound happy.

"What's the matter?" Rosie was good at noticing when her friends were feeling down. "Don't tell me — your brother!"

"You got it. He brought Drake and Ronny home after ski practice and they were torturing me about our invention. Ronny was jumping around in it, pretending to be a dog."

"Ronny Filmore isn't smart enough to be a dog!" Rosie declared. "Where are they?"

"Lifting weights, of course." Jon flexed his muscles and pretended to admire his physique in a mirror. Rosie laughed and joined in the pantomime, pretending to lift huge, heavy weights over her head. Mogul ran around them, trying to figure out what kind of new game they were playing.

"I don't want to go inside yet," Jon said. "Do you mind if we just hang out here for a while?"

"I don't mind," Rosie replied. "What do you want to do?"

"Well, I have an idea. It's something I've been wanting to try. Come with me."

Jon opened the door to the garage and disappeared inside. A few moments later he emerged with an ancient, rusty red sled and a piece of heavy rope.

"Is this an invention or a game?" Rosie asked, eyeing the old sled.

"A little of both. But wait — I need one more thing."

Jon hunted around in the garage again until he found the leather dog harness he had used when first taking Mogul to dog training.

"Okay," Rosie said with a laugh. "I give up!"

"Well, remember when I read that book all about Bernese Mountain Dogs?"

"Sure." Rosie shrugged. "They originally came from Switzerland, right?"

"Right. And they were bred to be working dogs. They were used to pull farm carts."

"Really?" Rosie asked. "Are they that strong?"

"Stronger than Drake and Ronny will ever be, even if they lift weights for the next hundred years! And Berners love to work — they have so much energy!"

"So you want Mogul to pull this old sled that you haven't played with since you were about six?" Rosie asked.

"It's just an experiment. I've never really seen Mogul do anything that you'd actually call work. But I know he's strong. I'd just like to find out if he carries the traits he was supposedly born with."

"Okay, let's try it," Rosie agreed. Her inventor's imagination was easily sparked.

The two friends set to work. First they gently fastened the harness on Mogul, who didn't seem to mind. He looked eager for whatever fun might be coming his way. Next Rosie tied the rope to the sled and threaded it through Mogul's harness. She

was good with knots — something Jon had always admired about her.

"There," Rosie said. "That should do it. Now what?"

Jon looked around. "Well, how about if I go stand over there by the trees and call Mogul. Then we can see how he does with the sled."

"Good idea," Rosie agreed. She knelt down and petted Mogul, while Jon jogged to the trees, about a hundred yards away. Mogul watched Jon go, eager to join him. But Rosie distracted the dog until Jon was in place.

"Come!" Jon called, kneeling down and holding his arms out to Mogul.

Mogul took off running, pulling the sled with apparent ease. To Rosie, it looked as if the dog didn't even notice the extra weight behind him. Mogul came to a stop in front of Jon, barely even panting.

"Good boy!" cried Jon. "What a good boy! You're so strong, aren't you?" He hugged Mogul and petted his back.

Rosie joined them, yelling with excitement. "He did it! He's a true Berner!"

Jon started to remove Mogul's harness but then stopped. He stared at the sled for a moment, realizing he needed to conduct a second step of the experiment. "I think we should try it again, but put some weight in the sled."

"Why?" asked Rosie.

"Because if Mogul lived on a farm in Switzerland and was pulling a cart, it would have something heavy in it, like wood or grain, maybe."

"You're right. But what could we use?" Rosie looked around the Ziller property. "How about some firewood?"

"That would work. Or how about a bag of rock salt from the garage?" Al Ziller used the salt to keep people from slipping on the icy path from his shop to the house. "Can you help me lift it?"

Rosie and Jon went back to the garage and together lifted the fifty-pound bag of salt and carried it over to the sled.

"Whew!" said Jon. "That's heavy!"

Rosie straightened her back and laughed. "If Mogul can pull this load, I'll *really* be impressed."

Once again, the two inventors repeated their experiment. Jon ran to the trees and yelled for Mogul to come. And once again, Mogul pulled the sled with apparent ease. The extra fifty pounds seemed to make little difference. Head held high, Mogul came to a stop in front of Jon.

Jon whistled through his teeth in appreciation. "Good boy! That was amazing, Mogul!"

Jon and Rosie marveled at the dog's strength as they unhooked the rope and removed Mogul's harness. Mogul looked at the two expectantly, as if to say, "That was fun — what's next?"

"That was incredible!" said Rosie. "Mogul *did* seem to be happy pulling that sled."

"I know," Jon said thoughtfully, rubbing Mogul's ear. "But the thing is — in modern life, there really isn't much work for dogs to do."

Rosie turned this over in her mind. "True," she

agreed, after a moment. "I suppose if you had small kids around, Mogul could pull them on the sled."

"I guess. But even if we lived on a farm, we'd use machines and equipment. We wouldn't need a dog to pull a cart around the farm."

"Do you think that makes working dogs sad?" Rosie wondered. "Or do you think they even know enough to realize that they don't have work to do?"

"I don't know," Jon admitted. "It's a good question. But I bet Mogul would love it if he could do something important for the people he loved."

"That's the difference between cats and dogs," Rosie said. "Cats only think about what *you* can do for *them*!"

Jon cracked up, imagining harnessing a cat to a wagon. "I've never heard of a working cat!"

"Race you up the hill!" Rosie called out suddenly. She zoomed off up the snowy incline, her hair flying behind her. Jon followed her, Mogul right at his heels.

When they reached the top of the hill, they looked down at the valley below, leaning over to catch their breath. For a moment, Jon felt a surge of pure happiness. He was outdoors with his best friend and his dog, surrounded by the natural beauty of the Rocky Mountains.

For that brief space of time, Jon forgot about spilling milk and losing control of the drill. He forgot about being skinny, and being younger, and feeling like a nerd around Eric and his rowdy friends.

Right then, the world seemed full of possibilities.

FIVE

The Invention Convention

The loudspeaker in the Peak Elementary School gym crackled and buzzed. Then Mrs. Hart, the principal, announced the beginning of the annual Invention Convention.

"Ladies and gentlemen," she began, "welcome to our yearly celebration of young inventors. I invite all of you to walk around the gym and visit each of the exhibitions. Talk to the inventors and ask questions. I think you'll be as impressed as I am with their intelligence and creativity."

When the principal finished speaking, the crowd in the gym came alive. Parents and friends quickly spread out to view the thirty inventions, which were arranged in a circle around the edges of the room. The four expert judges clutched their clipboards, ready to begin their official duties.

"Who are the judges?" Jon asked Rosie. "Do you know any of them?"

Rosie looked at the printed program in her hand. "It says here that one is a scientist at the state college, one is a computer expert from a big company, one works in research for the government, and the last one is actually an inventor who flew all the way out here from a company in Chicago!"

"Now I'm really nervous," Jon whispered. They stood next to each other and watched the frenzy of activity around them.

"Me too," Rosie admitted. "I keep thinking we forgot something."

Jon looked around at their exhibit to double-check. They had mounted a series of color photographs of the Wet Pet Splat Mat on a large piece of white cardboard, along with printed descriptions of how the invention had progressed. They also had a three-page written report that detailed the entire construction process. On the table, Rosie had arranged samples of all their building materials. And the actual box stood before them on the floor.

"I think we remembered everything," Jon said.

"Except for Mogul," Rosie added, laughing.

"My mom should be here any minute." Jon checked the big clock on the wall of the gym. It was nine-thirty on Saturday morning.

The judges of the Invention Convention had agreed to a one-time-only live demonstration of the Wet Pet Splat Mat at exactly ten o'clock A.M. Jon's mom would be arriving any minute with Mogul, a couple of buckets for water, and a bunch of old towels.

"I'm glad we finally convinced Mrs. Hart to let Mogul inside the school," Rosie said. "Imagine how hard it would be to try to explain our invention and not *show* it."

"I know," Jon agreed. "Ours is different from

most of the other entries. I mean, take Jack Finster's invention: a new kind of cup holder for the car. He can just put the whole thing out on his table, and everyone who comes by will understand what it is."

Rosie nodded her head vigorously. "Or how about Lisa and Sarah. Their invention smoothes crumpled dollar bills so they can be used in vending machines. That's pretty easy to demonstrate.

"But Mrs. Hart didn't think it would work out to have Mogul here all day, shaking water all over everything." Rosie sighed dramatically. "She's very conservative!"

Jon laughed at Rosie's joke, all the while keeping his eye on the clock. "Knowing Mogul, it probably wouldn't have worked out. Can't you just see him running around in here, knocking over displays with his tail?"

"I just hope he behaves for the demonstration," Rosie added.

Just then, several people stopped by their table

to look at the pictures and the written report. Rosie and Jon stood at attention, ready to answer questions.

"How'd you come up with the idea?" an older woman asked, smiling sweetly.

"All inventions start out with a need," Jon explained.

"And Jon had a need to keep his dog from messing up the house every time he went inside," put in Rosie.

"My mom was getting pretty tired of the wet and muddy tracks," explained Jon. "I'm trying to keep her happy."

"Good idea!" said the woman. "And good luck!" She moved quickly to the next exhibition.

"She didn't stay long," Jon observed, feeling disappointed.

"Oh, she probably has cats!" Rosie said, looking on the bright side as always. "Hey! There's your mom!"

Jon turned and spotted his mother, signaling to him from the door of the gym. "I'll be right back. You take charge here while I go get Mogul."

"Aye-aye!" Rosie said, saluting her partner.

Jon joined his mom by the door. "Where's Mogul?"

"Still in the car. I thought you could bring him in while I carry the rest of the things."

"And where's Dad? I thought he was bringing Eric over before they went to ski practice."

"He was," Bonnie began, "but Eric had a little accident."

"What happened?"

"Getting into the car, he slipped on some ice and fell. He hurt his wrist, and Dad took him over to Doctor French to get an X ray."

"Oh," Jon said, his heart sinking. "Is Eric okay?"

"I think so, honey. We'll know soon. Are you disappointed?"

"Yeah," Jon admitted slowly. "I really wanted Dad and Eric to see the demonstration."

"I know. It's such an exciting day for you. But I brought the video camera, so they can watch it later."

"It's not the same thing," Jon said. "It's not as good as being here. I mean, we don't just video-tape Eric's races — we go to them!"

"Eric didn't slip on purpose, Jon."

"I know. Look, I'd better go get Mogul."

All the way to the car, Jon felt disappointment stinging him like a swarm of bees. He knew Eric's fall had been an accident, but *why*? he wondered. *Why* did it seem as if Eric and his dad were never around when Jon had a chance to show them that he was special, too?

"Hey, Mogul!" Jon called, opening the door of the car. Mogul sprang out, dragging his leash between his legs. Jon grabbed the leather handle to make sure Mogul didn't take off in excitement. "Stay, Mogul, stay!"

Jon proudly led his dog inside the gym, while Bonnie carried the rest of the supplies and the video camera.

"Oh, look!" said Bonnie. "There are Rosie's parents and both of her sisters."

Sure enough, the entire Johnson clan surrounded Rosie at their table. "Hey, your whole family made it," Jon said.

"Can you believe it?" Rosie smiled. "They actually left someone else in charge of the restaurant for half an hour!"

"That's great," Jon responded. He tried to keep the twinge of envy he felt from showing in his voice. "Looks like it's almost time."

"Hey, Jon," said Rosie's oldest sister, Polly, "where's Eric? Is he coming?"

"He was supposed to, but he slipped and hurt his wrist."

"Oh, no!" Polly cried. "Is he okay? Will he still be able to ski?"

Jon shrugged and tried to smile. "I don't really know yet."

"That's terrible!" Polly continued. "He's the best skier Peak has ever had! Everyone in this town adores Eric!"

Jon stared at Polly, not sure what to say. He

didn't really feel like talking about Eric and besides, he needed to concentrate on the Wet Pet Splat Mat.

Luckily, Mrs. Hart interrupted with another announcement. "Ladies and gentlemen, in ten minutes we'll be having a demonstration at table number sixteen. This will be your only chance to see Jon Ziller and Rosie Johnson show their unique invention, using a real animal!"

A murmur of excitement rose from the crowd, and Jon's heart began beating faster. "Can you help me, Mom?"

"Sure, honey! What shall I do?"

"If you could lay out these towels, I'll pour the dirt on top. And then we'll splash the whole thing with water."

"I'll get the box ready," Rosie said, pulling it out in front of the table.

Mogul stood by Jon's side, distracted by the huge crowd of people moving around him. Jon noticed that the dog was panting, so he filled a bowl with water. Mogul lapped it up happily, then looked around, alert and curious.

The judges made their way to Jon and Rosie's table, along with a throng of observers. Jon spread dirt from a bucket over the old towels and then splashed the dirt with water until it formed a thin coating of mud.

"Are you ready, students?" Mrs. Hart asked.

Jon and Rosie nodded, and Mogul tried to squirm around the table.

"Are you ready, judges?" Mrs. Hart asked.

The judges nodded, poising their pens above their clipboards and watching Jon and Rosie intently. Jon's mother readied her video camera and Rosie cleared her throat to speak.

"Hello," Rosie said, smiling to the crowd. "I'm Rosie Johnson and this is my partner, Jon Ziller. Our invention is called the Wet Pet Splat Mat and it's designed to dry off your dog before he can track mud and water inside."

Jon admired how calm and confident Rosie

sounded, and how well she spoke in front of a crowd. He knew he was too nervous to talk, so he was grateful for Rosie's skill.

"And now," she continued, "Jon is going to demonstrate by having his dog, Mogul, get wet and muddy and then step inside our box."

Some of the people laughed as they realized what was about to happen, and at least a dozen small children pushed to the front of the crowd, hoping for a closer look at the mud and the dog.

"Mogul, come!" said Jon, stepping over to the muddy towels, laid end to end to form a long path. He dangled one of Mogul's favorite toys, a yellow plastic octopus, from the far end of the towels. From the other end, Mogul watched the toy intently, and then took several steps toward it.

But just then, the loudspeaker crackled and Mogul jumped with surprise. The leash snapped out of Jon's hand and Mogul was loose!

Jon watched helplessly as Mogul raced around the gym, weaving among groups of people and barking loudly. Everyone laughed at the sight of the large dog, running through the gym dragging his leash.

"He's scared!" Jon whispered to Rosie.

"Oh, no!" cried Rosie.

"We're in trouble!" Jon took a breath. "I'll try to catch him."

"Don't worry," Rosie said. "I'll keep the crowd entertained."

Jon ran after Mogul while Rosie stepped out front once again. "Ladies and gentlemen, please give us just a moment. As you know, dogs can be unpredictable at times, and that's just one more reason for the Wet Pet Splat Mat. Once your dog has used our invention, it won't matter if he runs all over the house. He'll be clean and dry, and your carpets will be safe!"

Jon finally caught up with Mogul and brought him safely back to the muddy towels. He was grateful for Rosie's ability to think and talk quickly. The judges looked a little confused, but they laughed along with the crowd.

"Come, Mogul," said Jon. And this time Mogul

went right for the toy, walking across the muddy towels to reach it.

"Sit!" said Jon. Mogul took the yellow toy in his mouth and plopped down.

"Good boy!" Jon said, petting his dog.

"Now," Rosie announced, "Jon will splash Mogul with just a bit more water so that the demonstration will be as realistic as possible."

John took a dish of warm water and lightly splashed it over Mogul's legs and paws. Mogul, who was used to baths, didn't react much except to stand up and begin to shake. But Jon quickly led the wet and muddy dog inside the box.

Once inside, Jon told Mogul to sit, and Mogul obeyed.

"You see," said Rosie, "the special sponge covering on the floor will absorb water and mud. You might want to give your pet a little treat while he dries."

Jon offered Mogul a biscuit, which the dog eagerly accepted and munched.

"By the time your dog is finished with his treat,

his paws will be nice and dry. Jon will demonstrate by spreading a clean white towel outside the
box."

Jon unfolded the towel and opened the hinged
door of the box.

"Come," he said to Mogul. Mogul looked up at
Jon and then stepped out of the box and onto the
white towel. Then Jon picked up the towel and
held it up for all to see. It was still clean! No
muddy paw prints!

"Wow!" said a voice from the crowd.

"Cool!" said someone else. "It works!"

"And that concludes our demonstration," said
Rosie.

The crowd applauded, and Jon felt his face
flush with happiness. He knelt down and gave
Mogul a big hug. "You were great!" he said. "You
really helped us out!"

Bonnie hugged her son and patted Mogul's
head. "That was terrific! I'm so proud of you!"

Suddenly Rosie and Jon were surrounded by
family and friends and well-wishers from the

crowd. One man even asked Jon if they would build a box for him to buy! Jon hadn't felt this happy in a long time. If only his dad and Eric could have been there, the moment would have been perfect. If only they had been there to hear people clapping and cheering for *him*!

"Do you think we have a chance of winning?" Rosie whispered.

"I don't know," said Jon. "And we have to wait to find out — all the way until Monday morning, when Mrs. Hart announces the winners at school."

"Well, it was a blast, anyway! And Mogul was so great."

"Yeah," Jon teased, "your cats would never do that!"

Rosie gave Jon an elbow in the side and smiled at him. "But cats don't get muddy," she reminded him. "They're very clean and quiet."

Suddenly Jon spotted Eric's friend Ronny heading directly toward him.

"What's *he* doing here?" Jon asked Rosie.

"He's probably coming over to congratulate

us!" Rosie just couldn't stop herself from thinking the best of people.

"Somehow I don't think so," Jon disagreed.

And sure enough, Ronny wasn't interested in Jon or Rosie or their invention.

"I just heard about Eric," he said. "Polly told me. Do you know anything yet? Is he hurt? He can't be hurt, man! Our biggest team race is coming up! And we can't win without Eric! The whole town is depending on him!"

Jon shook his head and looked down at Mogul. "I don't know anything yet, but my mom said she doesn't think it's serious."

He was thinking, *Why does everything always have to be about Eric?*

SIX

Snowy Sunday

"Wow, Mom! You look nice!" Jon said. "Are you leaving now?"

Bonnie nodded and smoothed her brown velvet dress. "The wedding starts at one o'clock and then the reception will probably last until five or six." Bonnie and Al were attending the wedding of one of Bonnie's coworkers and would be gone most of the afternoon. Eric would be in charge while their parents were away — which didn't exactly thrill Jon. He was still feeling disappointed that Eric and his dad had missed yesterday's Invention Convention.

Though he was glad that Eric's wrist was just fine, it didn't help knowing that they had missed his event for nothing. The doctor who had examined Eric told them that, at worst, Eric had merely bruised a bone and wouldn't require any treatment. Sometimes, Jon thought, his dad over-reacted to Eric's potential injuries.

Eric walked in from the kitchen, eating a bowl of cereal and looking at the newspaper. "Hey, Jon, there's a basketball game on at two. We could watch it together."

"Sure." Jon shrugged. Even though he didn't really like watching basketball, it was nice of Eric to ask. He figured that, in his own weird way, Eric was trying to make up for missing Jon's big day.

"Now, don't watch television all day," Bonnie reminded them. "You need to finish your homework. And there's a pot of soup on the stove for later."

"Don't worry," Eric assured her. "We'll be fine. We won't watch too much television, and we'll finish our homework. Right, Jon?"

"Right!" Jon promised. "Besides, I plan to play with Mogul. He deserves it after all his hard work yesterday."

Then Al came downstairs, wearing a suit and tie. This was a vast change from his usual attire of jeans, sweats, and old flannel shirts. Mogul stationed himself at Al's heels, trying to sniff the new leather of Al's shiny black shoes.

Jon thought his father looked like a movie star with his hair slicked back and his fancy clothes. *Will I ever look like that?* he wondered. *Will I ever be a grown-up and wear a suit?*

Al straightened his tie. "You guys take care of each other. We'll check in with you in a couple of hours, okay?"

"Okay." Eric nodded. "Have a good time!"

Jon waved to his parents from the living room window and watched as they drove away. He noticed that it had begun to snow lightly — big, fluffy flakes that drifted down and seemed to disappear before landing.

"Hey, Eric — it's snowing."

Eric glanced out the window and shouted, "Yes! We need some fresh snow! We haven't had any new snow in weeks!"

"It's pretty," Jon said, studying the pattern of a snowflake clinging to the window. The fact that no two snowflakes ever had the same pattern of crystals still amazed Jon.

"Who cares if it's pretty — it means great skiing!"

That's all you care about, Jon thought. *As brothers, we're as different from each other as two snowflakes.*

"So — want to watch the game?" Eric reached for the remote control. "Or do you have homework?"

"Actually, because of the Invention Convention, our teachers didn't give us any homework this weekend."

"Cool," Eric said. "Hey, I'm sorry we missed the invention thing. Mom said you did really great."

"Thanks." Jon smiled. It was nice of Eric to finally say something.

"So, did you win or what?"

"I'll know tomorrow when I get to school."

"Bummer! I don't think I could stand waiting for two days to find out if I won at something."

"Well, the judges have to go over their scores, and I guess that takes them a while. They had thirty inventions to look at."

"At a ski race, you know right away if you've won," Eric said. "That's the beauty of it. Instant winner!"

Jon just nodded. How could he explain to Eric that nothing was instant with inventions? Some inventors worked for decades on one project. Some gave their entire *life* to perfecting an invention.

But Eric was already engrossed in the basketball game, shouting encouragement to the televised players. He didn't even notice when Jon slipped his coat on and took Mogul outside. The snow had increased to a steady fall, now coating the driveway and the roof of the house.

Mogul ran at full speed, dipping his nose in and out of the wet snow and skidding down the driveway. Jon took a bright green tennis ball out of his pocket and tossed it to his dog.

"Go get it!" he shouted. "Go!"

Mogul ran and snapped the ball between his jaws. Then he brought it back to Jon and dropped it at his feet.

"Good boy!" Jon laughed. "Here you go!"

They played with the ball until Mogul was tired and panting. Then Jon opened the garage door and brought out his sled. As an afterthought, he also grabbed Mogul's leather harness, thinking it might be fun to see if Mogul would pull him on the sled.

But just as Jon was fitting Mogul's harness, Eric came outside, wearing his cross-country ski boots and carrying his skis and poles. "What are you up to?"

"Just playing with Mogul. Game over?"

"Halftime," said Eric. "Wow! This snow is excellent."

"I know," Jon agreed. "Mogul loves it."

"Hey, I have a great idea." Eric took a container of wax from his pocket. He began to apply the wax carefully, concentrating on the surface of his skis.

"What?" Jon asked, already knowing what Eric would propose.

"Let's go skiing."

"Why would you want me to go? You know I'm not very good."

"I'll help you. This snow is perfect."

Jon shrugged. It never seemed to work out when Eric tried to help him ski. He always became impatient and left Jon behind, which frustrated Jon and embarrassed him.

"Want to?" Eric pressed. "Come on, it'll be fun."

"I don't want to," Jon said. "I'll stay here."

"You can't. Mom doesn't want me to leave you alone. You know that!"

"I won't tell her," Jon argued. "I'll just stay here and play with Mogul."

"Mogul loves to come skiing! Don't you, boy?"

It was true — Mogul did love to trail along when anyone in the family went cross-country skiing. In fact, just the sight of Eric's skis was already sending Mogul into a fit of excitement. He paced around Eric, sniffing the wax and wagging his tail like crazy.

"We'll just go for a little bit," urged Eric. "Half an hour. Then we'll come back and eat soup. Hey — I'll even wax your skis!"

Jon realized he was about to go skiing, whether he wanted to or not. There was no hope of changing Eric's mind once he made a plan. "Okay, okay. But only for half an hour. And you can't make fun of the way I ski."

"I never do that!" Eric protested.

"Only all the time," Jon countered.

"Just trying to give you some brotherly advice. I wish *I* had a totally cool older brother who could teach *me* things."

It's not always as good as it sounds, Jon thought. But he didn't say it out loud. He didn't want to fight with Eric.

"Get your gear," Eric said. "I'll work on your skis."

Jon went inside, leaving Mogul to do his dance of anticipation around Eric. In the coat closet he dug out his wool hat, ski gloves, goggles, and his backpack with emergency supplies. Jon's father insisted that the boys carry their outdoor survival kits when skiing in the mountains around their home.

"You never know what could happen," Al always said. "Even if you're only a few minutes from home."

Jon peered inside the backpack to see what was there. He found a flashlight, a lighter, a whistle, a space blanket made of lightweight, insulated material, a Swiss army knife, a flare, some rope, a clump of bungee cords, two granola bars, a tin cup, and a water bottle. Jon filled up the water bottle at the kitchen sink, and returned it to his backpack.

Eric had finished waxing both sets of skis and was stepping into his own pair of racers. "What's with the backpack?"

"Dad always tells us we have to take the survival gear," Jon reminded him.

Eric laughed at his little brother as he put his

hands through the straps of his poles. "We're just going down by Fig Creek. It's not like we're heading into the wilderness for a week!"

"So?" Jon shot back. "I might get hungry or thirsty."

"You crack me up, Mr. Junior Forest Ranger!"

"Fine, Mr. Tough Guy. Don't come to me when you're thirsty."

Jon didn't care if Eric teased him. He knew it would make their dad happy that he'd remembered the most important rule of being outdoors in the mountains: *Be prepared!*

"Let's go!" Eric called. "Come on, Mogul!"

Eric skied off, easily and gracefully. Mogul ran after him, trotting happily in the tracks made by Eric's skis.

Jon suddenly realized that Mogul was still wearing the leather harness, but there was no time to remove it now. And Mogul wouldn't even notice he was wearing it — he was thrilled to be going on an adventure with the boys!

As always, Jon struggled to keep up with Eric.

And often he struggled just to keep his balance. He simply didn't comprehend the rhythm of cross-country skiing. You had to use your right arm and left leg to move forward, followed by the left arm and right leg. The coordination of two poles and two skis wasn't the most natural thing in the world. Jon preferred snowshoeing, which he found almost as easy as walking

But Eric loved the speed and glide of cross-country skiing, and Jon had to admit that his brother was fun to watch. He made the sport look effortless, though Jon knew the hours and hours of training it took each week for Eric to stay strong and conditioned.

Though Eric was only a dozen strides ahead of Jon, Mogul ran back and forth between the brothers.

"You want us to stay together, don't you, Mogul?" Jon realized.

Mogul barked in reply and headed off toward Eric. It made Jon smile to know that Mogul was trying to keep them from getting separated.

"Wait up!" Jon called, panting with the effort of trying to catch up to his brother.

Eric stopped and turned around. He watched Jon struggle up behind him.

"Glide!" Eric called. "You're working too hard!"

"You're telling me!" Sweat trickled down Jon's neck.

"It's that stupid backpack!" Eric shot back. "It's weighing you down!"

Finally, Jon caught up to his brother. "Wow! Look how pretty everything is." Jon stared out at the snow-covered trees and the frozen creek beside them.

"Don't stop now," Eric urged. "You're just getting warmed up."

"But it's so beautiful!"

"Never look behind," said Eric. "Just keep your eye on the destination."

"What *is* our destination?" Jon wasn't sure if he wanted to hear the answer.

"That ridge up there, above the creek."

"You mean — we're going *uphill*?"

"Sure." Eric shrugged. "If you like views, there's an awesome one from up there."

"But I'm terrible at going uphill," Jon protested.

"I'll show you. Easy as pie! Watch!"

Eric's voice was like a bell ringing out in the quiet of the mountains. There was so much joy and confidence in it. It was contagious, and Jon knew he would continue — as always — to follow his big brother's tracks in the snow.

Wherever they might lead.

SEVEN

Eric Disappears

"Just watch me for a second!" Eric called back to Jon. "I'm using the herringbone position to climb the hill."

Jon and Mogul waited at the bottom of the snowy incline and watched as Eric made a wide *V* with his skis. He spread the tips far apart, keeping his heels together.

"You have to angle the bottom edges of your skis into the snow," shouted Eric. "And drop your knees down. Then plant your poles on the outside of the skis, and just start walking."

"Easy for *him* to say," Jon muttered, trying to imitate Eric's stance.

Mogul ran a few yards ahead, then looked eagerly back at Jon. "Come on," he seemed to be saying. "You can do it!"

"Okay," Jon said. "I'll give it my best try."

He positioned his skis as Eric had showed him. So far so good. He planted his poles and took a few tentative steps forward.

Mogul barked more encouragement, running back and forth between the two boys. Jon decided to try his brother's technique of focusing only on the destination. He stared straight ahead and imagined the breathtaking view he would soon have of the Peak Valley.

But suddenly he started slipping backward. "Oh, no! Dang it!"

Eric turned and skied back down to Jon. "Your *V* isn't wide enough. You need to spread your skis farther apart."

Jon clenched his teeth. "Okay. Thanks."

"You're doing fine," Eric told him. "You can make it."

Jon nodded and adjusted his skis once more. Mogul stood patiently beside him.

"And it helps if you don't let your weight sit too far back. Try to find a balance."

Jon leaned forward a bit more and tried again. To his happy surprise, it worked much better this time! Eric really knew what he was talking about! Jon felt a small glow of accomplishment as he made his way up thc hill, staring at Eric's back and repeating to himself, "I can do it, I can do it, I can do it."

Once again, Eric turned and skied back to Jon. "How're you doing?"

"Better. Thanks for the advice."

"Hills are definitely a challenge. But they're also a blast!"

"If you like torture," Jon joked. "If you like the feeling that your lungs are about to burst."

"If you get tired, just take a break and use a sidestep."

"I think I will." Jon turned so that the right side of his body faced the hill and his skis were parallel. He took a series of right-left steps up the hill, giving his breathing a chance to slow down.

"Hey," said Eric, "I think I'll head on up to the top, if you don't mind. How about if I meet you in a few minutes?"

"Okay," Jon agreed. But he was thinking, *This is what always happens. I slow you down and you take off and leave me in the dust!*

"Just take your time — you're doing great," Eric called over his shoulder.

"Where will you be exactly?"

"On the ridge — to the right of that clump of evergreens. Okay?"

"Okay!" Jon called. To Mogul he said, "We'll just take our time, boy. We'll let Mr. Hotshot be the winner."

Mogul dashed after Eric, but then came right back to Jon's side. The dog seemed to think he was playing an energetic game of hide-and-seek!

"How come," Jon said to Mogul, "you're not even panting hard, while I can barely breathe? How do you explain that?"

Mogul barked and zipped up the hill once again.

Slowly, Jon made his way to the top. He took turns using the herringbone and sidestep until, finally, he made it. He took a huge gulp of air and blew it out with relief and satisfaction.

"Eric!" he shouted. "I made it! I'm here!"

But Eric didn't answer.

"Eric!" Jon shouted again, this time using the full power of his voice. But Eric didn't answer.

"That's weird," Jon said to his dog. "He said he'd be at the ridge, to the right of the trees. Now where is he?"

Jon skied over to the trees, hoping to find Eric playing a game of hide-and-seek with him. But Eric wasn't there. Mogul sniffed around the trunks of the evergreens, his nose buried in the snow. Jon stared down the opposite side of the hill. It was densely covered with trees, so it was impossible to see much of anything. If Eric was down there, he wasn't answering.

Jon cupped his mouth with his hands and aimed his voice down the tree-lined slope. "Eric! Eric!"

His own voice came echoing back to him. Jon felt a tremor of alarm.

Where was his brother? And what should he do now? Wait? Look around? Go back home? Why didn't Eric stay where he was supposed to? Why did he always leave Jon behind?

"Hey, Mogul," Jon said, trying to keep his voice light. "Has it been snowing this hard all along? Or is it getting worse all of a sudden?"

It did seem that in a short time the snow had changed from a gentle drifting to a real winter storm. And a cold wind whipped across the ex-posed ridge. While climbing the hill, Jon had felt so hot and sweaty. But now, he shivered with cold.

"Let's have a snack," Jon suggested to Mogul. "That way we'll have energy to ski home when Eric finally shows up."

He removed his backpack and set it down in the snow. Taking off one glove, he dug around un-til he found a granola bar and the bottle of water. He took a long drink, and then split the granola bar in two. "Here you go, boy." He offered half to Mogul. Mogul licked Jon's bare hand and then gently took his treat.

Jon and his dog chewed their snack in silence. The wind swirled snow into their faces. When they were finished, Jon heaved the backpack onto his shoulders again and slapped his hands together to try and warm them up.

"I think," Jon said out loud, "that we should stay here. When you get separated in the mountains, you should just stay where you are and not risk getting more lost. Not that I'm lost — Eric is the one who seems to be lost. I'm sure he'll turn up soon."

But Jon didn't feel nearly as confident as his words sounded. He was getting cold — and worried. He wished with all his heart that Eric would just appear so they could go home and get warm. He thought longingly of the pot of vegetable soup his mom had left on the stove. And he thought about sitting in front of the fire with Mogul in his toasty house, safe from the storm that was obviously picking up speed as it moved across the valley.

Jon looked at Mogul, who was never bothered by the cold. "I wish I had your double coat. Fur must be a lot warmer than man-made fibers. Hey, maybe I should invent a coat made of dog hair. Mom would like that — finally, a use for all the hair you leave around the house."

Jon stamped his skis in the snow and blew clouds of breath into the air. He wondered what to do next. Then he spotted a nice fat stick lying in the snow. He put his poles down and grabbed it.

"Hey, Mogul, go get it!" He tossed the stick toward the clump of trees and Mogul dashed after it.

Mogul brought the stick back in his mouth and dropped it at Jon's feet. Then Jon picked it up and tossed it again. He was amazed that his dog could find the stick again and again in the midst of blowing snow. They played catch for another few minutes. Mogul was having fun, but Jon was growing

frightened. Why had he ever agreed to go skiing with Eric?

Jon threw the stick once more, this time accidentally sending it over the ridge and down the tree-covered side of the hill. Mogul ran after it, half sliding down the steep, slippery ground.

"Mogul, come!" Jon shouted. He was afraid that Mogul would disappear, too. Then he would really be all alone. He shielded his eyes from the snow and tried to spot Mogul. He could hear the faint sounds of Mogul's jingling tags, but he couldn't see him at all.

"MOGUL!" he screamed. "COME BACK!"

Again, Jon could hear the tags clinking together. Now they were coming closer. "Mogul, come! Come back here!"

And then Mogul finally reappeared, his black coat a striking contrast to all the blowing white snow.

"Don't tell me you actually found the stick," Jon said, shaking his head. "You're a maniac!"

But when Mogul reached Jon's side, he didn't

have the stick at all. He had something else clenched between his jaws. It was covered with snow, but when he dropped it at Jon's feet, Jon recognized it immediately.

It was a blue ski glove.

And it belonged to Eric!

EIGHT

An Emergency Invention

Jon picked up Eric's glove and turned it over in his hands. His heart pounded wildly in his chest. Eric was in trouble! They had to find him, and quickly. The snow was almost blinding, and the temperature seemed to be dropping by the minute.

"What are we going to do?" Jon said to Mogul. His teeth chattered and his breath came in uneven bursts. But he tried not to panic. He knew he must do his best to stay calm and think clearly.

Mogul ran to Jon's side and leaned against him. It was what he always did when he sensed that Jon was upset. Jon knelt down awkwardly to take off his skis. If Eric was lost somewhere down the tree-covered slope, there was no way Jon could reach his brother wearing skis. He'd have to walk down, and carry his equipment.

As Jon unlatched his left ski from the binding, Mogul stood right beside him. Jon leaned over and buried his head in Mogul's soft fur, then threw his arms around his dog. The warmth of Mogul's coat was so comforting! The dog turned to lick Jon's face and Jon felt instantly better. He wasn't alone on the ridge of the mountain — he had Mogul with him! And together they would find Eric and get safely home.

Jon considered leaving his skis and poles behind, but then thought better of it. They might just come in handy if Eric's own equipment was broken or lost. Hooking the skis and poles together in one compact bundle, he settled them over his shoulder, above his backpack. Then he pulled his hat farther down over his ears and adjusted his goggles.

"Let's go," he said to Mogul, trying to sound brave. "Show me where you found the glove."

The instant Jon made his first move, Mogul

took off running down the slope, dodging trees. Jon lost sight of him, but tried not to worry. After all, Mogul had been running back and forth between the two boys all afternoon. Jon simply had to trust that his dog would return and lead him to Eric.

But it was difficult trying to walk down the hill. In some places the snow was so deep that Jon's feet sunk unexpectedly, causing him to lose his balance. And it didn't help that he had a backpack, skis, and poles to carry. Not to mention the fact that cross-country ski boots offered little in the way of traction.

"Eric!" he called. "Eric! Can you hear me? Mogul? Mogul!"

But the only sound Jon heard was his own eerie and hollow echo. Why didn't Eric answer? Where was he? And was he all right?

Jon slipped again, this time falling backward and landing on his shoulder. The skis and poles went flying. Jon felt tears sting his cheek. His shoulder hurt, and he was getting really frightened

now. What if he and Eric never found each other
and they both froze on the mountainside? What if
he never saw his mom and dad again? He wanted
to stay there in the snow and try to get warm. He
didn't know if he even had the energy to stand up.

But then Mogul returned, barking frantically
and nudging Jon to get up.

"What is it? Did you find Eric?"

Mogul barked again with new urgency. He ran
around Jon with a wild energy Jon couldn't ig-
nore.

"Okay, okay," Jon mumbled. "I'm coming. Just
let me stand up and find my stuff."

When he had recovered his skis and poles, Jon
turned to Mogul and took a deep breath. "I'll try to
keep going, but you have to stay with me."

Mogul obeyed and stayed just a few feet in
front of Jon, looking back every few seconds to
see if Jon was coming. Jon knew he should keep
yelling for his brother, even though his voice was
growing hoarse and tired.

"Eric!" he called. "Eric! Please! Talk to me, Eric!"

Suddenly a different sound echoed back. Jon froze in his tracks. Mogul barked in frustration, but Jon hushed him. "Quiet, Mogul. Listen!"

Jon called for Eric again. And this time he heard a faint reply.

"O-ver heeere!"

"That way!" Jon turned toward the voice. "Eric's over there."

Jon forgot how tired and cold and scared he was! He nearly ran through the trees, Mogul just ahead of him. He forgot about everything but reaching his brother. He took step after step through the heavy snow, panting from the physical exertion.

Following Mogul, Jon finally spotted a blur of red, which he guessed was Eric's ski parka.

"Eric!" he cried.

"Here!"

When Mogul and Jon reached Eric's side, they found him sitting in the snow with his back against a tree, nearly halfway down the slope. He had his gloveless hand tucked inside his coat. The

other hand covered a small gash on his forehead.

"Are you okay?" Jon asked, deeply relieved to see that his brother was alive and sitting up. "What happened?"

"I messed up my ankle and cut my head," Eric said slowly. Jon was shocked to realize that his big brother sounded hurt and scared, too. He couldn't remember a time when Eric had been anything but strong and confident — a winner and a hero.

"What happened?" Jon repeated. He kneeled down beside Eric, and Mogul crowded between them. "Where did you go?"

"It was stupid! When I saw that you were almost to the top of the hill, I decided to be a hot dog and ski down this side just a little ways. I figured that Mogul would keep running back and forth between us. Only I lost control and slid into a tree. I'm such a jerk!"

"You really scared me," Jon admitted. "I don't know what I would have done without Mogul. I never would have found you."

"I'm sorry," Eric said. He reached over and

touched Jon's arm. "I really am. It's totally my fault."

"Don't worry. It's going to be okay." Jon felt weird to be the one comforting Eric, instead of the other way around. But it also felt pretty good!

"Are you okay?" Eric asked. "Did you get hurt or anything?"

"Nah!" Jon said, giving a shrug. "I'm getting cold, though."

"Me too. But at least you're okay. Mom would kill me if I let anything happen to you. But let's face it — she's going to kill me, anyway."

"No, she won't. Don't worry about that right now."

"Actually," Eric continued, "it's Dad who will kill me."

"Why?"

"Because I think I really screwed up my ankle. I probably messed up my chance to race in New York. He's going to be so disappointed."

Jon felt suddenly protective of Eric. "You can't worry about that right now. We have to get out of this snow or we're going to freeze. How's your head?"

"I think the bleeding stopped," Eric said, taking his hand away from the wound.

"Oh, man." Jon didn't like the looks of the jagged cut covered with dried blood. "That must hurt!"

"Not as much as my ankle."

"Do you think it's broken?"

"I can't tell. But the thing is — I don't know if I can walk."

Jon was silent for a moment, trying to think about their options. Mogul hovered nearby, loyal as always.

"If Mogul were Lassie," Jon said, "we could send him back home to get help. But he won't go until we do." He tried to force a little laugh, but it didn't quite work.

Eric looked at Jon very seriously. "I think you and Mogul should try to get back home and call for help."

"I can't leave you here! No way!"

"But we can't both stay here," Eric said. "Someone has to go for help."

"There must be another option." Jon tried hard to think clearly. He was an inventor, after all! There had to be a creative solution to this problem. The boys had a need to get home. And a need for something was always the first step in any invention.

Jon suddenly remembered Eric's lost glove. "Here. Put this back on before your hand freezes. And I think you should eat a granola bar. You're going to need the energy."

Jon fished inside his backpack, finding the second granola bar and the half-filled water bottle. He tore off the wrapper and handed the bar to Eric. "Drink some water, too. You don't want to get dehydrated."

Eric chewed hungrily and finished off the water. "And to think I gave you grief for bringing your backpack and all that gear."

Jon's mind was racing now, slipping into invention mode. He took the silver space blanket out of his pack and wrapped it around Eric's shoulders. "This will keep you warm," he said. "I need a few minutes to figure things out."

"What do you mean?" Eric asked, his teeth chattering.

"I have an idea."

"An idea for what?"

"For getting us out of here!" Jon dumped the entire contents of his backpack onto the snow and took inventory. There wasn't a lot of equipment, but he did have some essential items. And he had the seeds of a plan in his mind.

Meanwhile, Mogul parked himself practically on top of Eric. It was as though he knew that the most helpful thing he could do at the moment was provide extra heat for Eric. But his eyes were on Jon, watching as Jon took Eric's skis and placed them near his own on the snow.

"What are you doing?" Eric sounded skeptical.

"Making a sled."

"A sled?" Eric repeated. "With what?"

"With the tools at hand. I'm an inventor, remember?"

Jon took his two skis and bound them together at the tip and heel with two bungee cords. Then he did the same with Eric's skis. He placed the two sets of skis about two feet apart in the snow, pointing up the slope like the blades of a sleigh. Then he bundled his poles together, opposite ends touching, and tied them together with their hand straps. He did the same with Eric's poles.

I hope this works, Jon thought.

"I don't get it, Jon. What are you thinking?"

"I'm thinking of a way to get you home. Now stop interrupting me!"

"Yes, sir!"

Jon thought it was funny to be giving his brother orders. It had always been the other way around. Now he only had to prove that his idea could work.

Using his Swiss Army knife, Jon cut a length of rope into several smaller sections. After crossing the two sets of poles to make an *X* between the skis, Jon tied a knot around the intersection of the poles. It wasn't as nice-looking as one of Rosie's knots, but it would hold. Then he slipped each corner of the *X* through the bungee cords at each end of the double skis.

"There!" he said. "The frame of the sled."

Then Jon took his empty backpack and anchored it with rope to the crossed poles, forming a seat. He covered the seat with the space blanket, for extra padding and warmth. He shook the frame several times to test for strength and endurance.

"That should hold you," he said to Eric. "Can you slide over here?"

Eric stared at him for a minute, his mouth hanging open.

"Come on! Unless you want to spend the night out here!"

Eric slid from the tree to the improvised seat, moaning with pain as he moved his injured ankle. Jon helped settle Eric onto the sled, gently placing his brother's feet on the tips of the double sets of skis. Mogul danced around the boys, sniffing the invention with great curiosity.

"Are you comfortable?" Jon asked.

"As comfortable as I can be at the moment."

"Don't drag your feet, it will slow us down. Now, do you feel steady on the seat?"

"Pretty much," Eric answered, shifting his weight a bit.

"Okay, now hold on while I test something." Jon moved behind his brother and placed his hands on Eric's back. Then he gently pushed. They lurched and then moved slowly forward.

"Yes!" Jon whispered. "Good!"

"You mean you're going to push me the rest of the way up the hill?" Eric asked. "You'll never make it. I must be double your weight!"

"I'm not finished yet! Give me a break!"

"Okay, Jon-O. I'm sorry."

Eric's voice was faint, and Jon noticed that his brother's face looked very pale. A light blue color tinged his lips. Jon knew it was time to go. *Now!*

"Mogul, come!" Jon called. And Mogul quickly

obeyed, coming around to Jon and looking up expectantly.

"Sit," Jon said, motioning for the dog to sit several feet in front of the sled. Jon threaded his last piece of rope through Mogul's harness and handed the ends to Eric. Mogul wiggled his tail happily. He knew what was coming. He was going to pull. He was going to work!

"You mean Mogul's going to pull me?" Eric asked.

"He's done it before," explained Jon. "Rosie and I harnessed him to that old sled at home and put a bag of salt in it and he pulled it around like it was nothing."

Eric groaned. "Oh, man! My ankle really hurts."

"Here's how this works," Jon explained, his voice full of confidence. "I'm going to run uphill once, to pack a trail in the snow. Then I'm going to push you from behind while Mogul pulls you up the hill. Once we're over the ridge, Mogul will pull you down the other side easily."

"I don't believe it," Eric sighed. "But let's give it a go."

"All you have to do is stay on the seat. Keep your balance and don't let Mogul drag you off. Plant your good leg hard against the ski, okay?"

"Okay," Eric agreed. Then he watched in amazement as his younger brother ran up the hill, pounding the snow down with his cross-country boots. Winded, Jon ran back to Mogul and Eric, giving the trail a second stamp for good measure.

"Ready?" Jon panted.

"Ready," said Eric.

"Good boy!" Jon patted Mogul's head. "We're counting on you to get Eric up this hill. You know what to do!"

Mogul tossed his head and looked back at both boys, eyes steady and calm. After checking the tension of all the ropes and cords, Jon shouted, "Go, Mogul! Go!"

Jon leaned into the hill while Mogul heaved forward, and the sled inched uphill. After a few minutes, Jon and Mogul found a steady rhythm of pushing and pulling, and things went more smoothly. It was hard work for both, but they kept their sights on the top of the hill.

"You okay?" Jon panted, trying not to lose his foothold in the snow.

"Yeah," Eric grunted. The pain was evident in his voice this time.

"Good boy!" Jon shouted to Mogul. "Good job!"

From behind, Jon could see Mogul's powerful legs straining with the weight of his load. His eyes filled with tears of pride at the willingness of his dog to take on such a difficult task. Jon thanked his lucky stars that he had unthinkingly put Mogul in the harness before they left on their skis.

But just then, the sled hit a buried rock.

The sled lurched and tumbled to the side, dumping Eric into the snow!

NINE

Safely Home

"Oh, no!" Jon cried. "Are you okay, Eric?"

Eric lay facedown in the snow, not moving. Mogul whined with worry and wagged his tail furiously. Jon ran over and kneeled down beside his brother.

"Are you hurt?"

Eric moaned and rolled over. He looked up at Jon, but didn't say anything. Then, strangely, he began to laugh. "We were going pretty well, weren't we?" He sputtered and wiped snow from his face. Then he laughed some more and tried to raise himself up on an elbow.

"Your leg really hurts, doesn't it?"

"Yeah," Eric admitted. "It's pretty bad."

"Can you get back on the sled? We need to

keep going." Jon looked up at the top of the hill, which was only a hundred yards away. But the winter sky was darkening, and soon the sun would completely disappear.

"I think I can." Eric sat up and scooted toward the sled, wincing with pain as he moved his bad leg. Jon put his arms around Eric's chest and helped pull him back onto the seat.

"There you go!" Jon hoped his voice sounded encouraging. He was terribly tired, and his muscles ached from pushing and walking. But he needed to be brave until they were safely home.

Mogul barked impatiently. Jon knew his dog wanted to keep going, too — he was probably dreaming of a big dish of food and a warm fire.

"I don't think we'll tip over again," Jon said. "We just hit a big rock that we couldn't see. We're almost to the top! Are you ready?"

"Ready. You're doing a great job, Jon."

"You think so?" Jon's voice rose in surprise.

"Definitely. I would never have thought of something like this."

Jon felt a flush of pride at his brother's unexpected compliment. It made him even more determined to get them all home safely.

"Go, Mogul! Let's go!"

For the next few minutes, no one spoke. Jon was huffing so hard the sound rang in his ears. Then Eric turned around and said, "You might think about making the seat a tad more comfortable. I think my backside is bruised!"

Jon and Eric shared a laugh at this, and for once, Jon felt very close to his brother. It was a feeling he hadn't had in a long time — not since Eric had become a serious athlete with little time for anything else.

"Look!" Jon shouted. "The ridge! We made it to the top!"

"Now it's downhill all the way," commented Eric.

"Mogul will be glad for that! He must be exhausted."

On top of the ridge, Jon looked down and spotted the Ziller house. The sight filled him with relief. He couldn't wait to get there! No smoke rose from the chimney, meaning the logs in the fireplace had long since burned down. He looked quickly at his watch and discovered that it was nearly five o'clock. They had been gone for hours. Their parents would be home soon, but Jon knew that Eric would need a doctor right away.

"Let's go," he urged Mogul, "Let's go home!"

Mogul pulled forward and the sled followed easily down the gentle incline. There was no need for Jon to push, but he stayed behind to make sure the sled didn't pick up speed and move too close to his dog. He thought about how he would get Eric to the hospital. He could call Rosie and see if anyone at her house could drive them into town. Failing that, he would call 911 and ask for an ambulance.

"Wheee!" Eric whooped. "This is a good ride!"

It did look like fun, Jon thought. The skis made for very fast runners. He couldn't wait to show his invention to Rosie and get her input on improving the design.

"Hold on tight!" Jon called. He didn't want

Eric to have any more unexpected tumbles in the snow. He knew enough basic first aid to realize that if Eric's ankle was broken, he should move his leg as little as possible. So far, Jon had tried not to focus on the extent of Eric's injury and what it could do to his skiing career. But now, worrisome thoughts came creeping into his mind. How would Eric manage if he couldn't ski? And what about their dad and all his dreams for Eric?

Mogul and Eric and the sled arrived home several moments before Jon, coming to a stop in front of the garage. Jon ran up and joined them, out of breath.

"We made it!" Eric called, looking back over his shoulder. "You did it!"

The brothers gave each other a high five. Jon wanted to collapse right there in the driveway, but he still had work to do. He unhooked the rope and harness from Mogul, giving his dog a big hug.

"Thank you, Mogul! You were awesome! An honor to your breed. Bernese Mountain Dogs rule!"

"I second that! Now, one problem, Jon. How am I going to get inside?"

"I thought about that. And I remembered that Dad has an old pair of crutches in the garage."

"From way back when he crashed *his* knee skiing?" asked Eric.

"Yeah — they're old. Wait here."

"Like father like son," muttered Eric.

Sure enough, Jon found the ancient wooden crutches in a corner of the garage, next to a box of old books and a flattened basketball. He brought them over to Eric and held one out horizontally.

"Hold on to this and I'll pull you up."

Slowly and painfully Eric managed to get to his feet and balance on one foot while Jon steadied the crutches. Then Jon ran ahead and opened the front door. Mogul dashed inside and went right for his water bowl in the kitchen. Eric inched his way through the door and over to the sofa.

"I'm going to call Rosie and see if her mom or sisters can drive us to the hospital," Jon explained. But Eric didn't answer. Now that he was safely home, he collapsed onto the sofa, done in by the pain and cold and the long ordeal. Jon covered his brother with an afghan and then ran to the kitchen to call Rosie.

No one answered at Rosie's house, even though Jon let the phone ring at least twelve times. He tried to remember where the wedding reception was that his parents were attending. He knew his mom had told all those details to Eric. Should he wake Eric and ask him? Or should he let him sleep?

Jon decided he'd better call an ambulance. What if Eric had other injuries that couldn't be seen? It was best not to take any chances. His fingers shook as he dialed 911. He'd never done that before, except to practice once at school with a pretend phone.

The woman who answered the phone was calm and friendly. She asked Jon a few questions, such as: Was his brother breathing? Was he bleeding? How long ago did the injury happen? Then she told him to keep Eric covered up and warm and that the ambulance would be there as soon as possible.

Jon was shaking when he put the phone down. Things felt very serious now. At times, the process of inventing the sled and getting Eric home had almost seemed like a game. But now, with an ambulance on its way to take his brother to the hospital, Jon was overwhelmed by the gravity of the situation.

"I wish Mom and Dad were here!" he said out loud. "Mogul? Where are you, boy?"

Mogul wandered in slowly from the living room and looked up at Jon. Jon was glad to see that Mogul was all right, but he could tell the dog was more tired than he had ever been. "Go back to sleep, boy. You earned it." Mogul dropped to the floor in front of the sink and curled into a tight ball.

He went into the living room and pulled the blanket tighter around Eric. Eric started and looked up at Jon. "Hey. How's it going?"

"Eric, an ambulance is coming. Can you remember where Mom and Dad are for the wedding reception?"

"At Rosie's parents' café," Eric mumbled.

"Of course!" Jon smacked his forehead. "That's why no one was home at Rosie's!"

He ran back to the kitchen and looked up at the list of numbers his mom kept posted by the phone. He located the number of the café and dialed it quickly. Polly, Rosie's sister, answered with a crisp "hello."

"This is Jon Ziller. Can I talk to my mom or dad, please? It's important."

"Sure," Polly said. "Hold on and I'll get them."

While Jon waited, he tried to think how to tell his parents what had happened without giving them a heart attack. But before he could decide, he heard his mom's worried voice.

"Jon, are you okay?"

"I'm fine, Mom. But Eric had an accident ski-ing. He hurt his ankle really badly."

"When? How?"

"Mom," Jon continued, "I had to call an ambulance. They're on the way. I think you and Dad should meet us at the hospital."

There was a moment of silence, and Jon could hear his mother's sharp intake of breath. "We'll be right there. You did the right thing to call us, Jon."

"Okay," Jon said. "See you at the hospital."

After what seemed like hours, but was only minutes, Jon heard the ambulance pull into the driveway. He was glad they didn't use the siren — his heart was pounding too fast already. He ran to the door and flung it open. A young man and woman dressed in paramedic uniforms came bustling inside. They smiled calmly at Jon, and he instantly felt better. Help had arrived!

Jon led them to Eric, and they went to work quickly. They checked Eric's blood pressure, temperature, and pulse, and examined his ankle and the cut on his forehead. Eric was awake but quiet and seemed to be trembling with cold.

Jon suddenly realized that Mogul hadn't even stirred when strangers came into the house. He hadn't barked or come over to stand protectively next to the boys when the paramedics arrived. *This is a first!* thought Jon.

As the woman cleaned Eric's cut, the man went outside and returned with a stretcher. Jon watched helplessly as they lifted his brother and strapped him down on the stretcher. They covered him with a blanket and carried him out to the back of the ambulance.

"Are you coming along?" the woman asked pleasantly.

"Am I allowed to?" Jon said.

"Sure. Where are your parents?"

"In town at a reception. I called them, and they're meeting us at the hospital."

"You've done a great job of handling things," complimented the woman. "You should feel really proud for staying calm and clearheaded in an emergency."

Jon wanted to smile, but he was too scared. He closed the door behind him, glancing back to make sure that Mogul was still asleep in front of the sink. He wished he could curl up next to his dog and sleep for hours.

But he had to see things through to the end.

While they waited for the doctors to finish Eric's X rays, Jon and his parents sat on the hard plastic chairs of the emergency room. Jon sipped a cup of hot chocolate from the vending machine and told the whole story for the second time.

"I can't believe you did all that yourself!" Bonnie exclaimed.

"I'm so impressed by you, son," said Al. "It's just mind-boggling to think that you figured out what to do, and you got Eric home."

"And that you called for help," Bonnie continued.

"Don't forget Mogul," Jon said. "He was the real hero. We never would have made it without Mogul pulling the sled. And he's the one who led me to Eric in the first place."

"I'll make him pancakes when we get home, to show our gratitude," Bonnie said. Pancakes were one of Mogul's favorite people foods.

"He'll like that." Jon smiled, thinking of Mogul gobbling up a bowl full of hot pancakes with butter.

"He's an amazing animal," Bonnie added. "We're lucky to have him as part of our family."

"I would never have known how to make a sled out of two pairs of skis and some rope," Al put in. "It just amazes me!"

Jon smiled and leaned against his mom. He was beyond tired now. He felt numb and heavy. But he was worried about his brother.

"Dad? What if Eric can't ski anymore?"

Al was quiet for a minute. Then he rubbed his hand across his forehead and turned to Jon. "Then we'll just have to be glad that he's safe and alive. And work on helping him heal."

"But I know how important it is to you, Dad."

"What's important?"

"Eric being a great skier like you were. Making you proud — making the whole town proud."

"Is that what you think?" Al's voice cracked a little, as if he were about to cry.

"Sure," Jon answered. "Eric's the pride of our family."

Al reached over and took Jon's hand. He squeezed it hard and then looked over at Bonnie. She shrugged and gave him a knowing smile.

"Boy," said Al. "I've really messed things up if I've made you think that your brother is the pride of the family."

"He is," Jon said simply.

"No, he isn't. Both of my sons are the pride of the family. I love you both so much. And I'm proud of *both* of you."

"But you have to admit, Dad, that Eric's a hero."

"Let me tell you something," Al said. He looked intently at Jon. "I want you to understand this. A hero is a person who acts unselfishly to benefit others. You are a hero today, Jon. You saved your brother's life. You acted in a caring and un-selfish way."

"And that ability is a lot more important than being skilled at a sport," Bonnie put in. "Being an athlete is great. But being a good person is best of all!"

"I'm sorry if I've been too focused on Eric's racing, son. And I'm sorry I missed your inventor's day at school. I feel really bad about that. I want to make it up to you, if you'll let me."

Jon leaned over to give his father a hug. He felt as though a heavy weight had been lifted from his shoulders. He felt warm, and light, and full of love for his family. And he admired his dad for being able to admit a mistake — that was pretty cool when a parent did something like that!

"Excuse me," said a tall woman in a white coat. "Are you the Zillers?"

"Yes," said Bonnie, standing up quickly.

"I'm Doctor Green. I'm afraid your son has a pretty bad break in his ankle."

"Oh, no!" whispered Jon, looking up at his dad.

"Everything is going to be fine," Al said, putting an arm around his son.

TEN

Jon Makes the Headlines!

On Monday, Jon was allowed to skip home-room to go to the hospital with his parents. He was eager to see how Eric was doing after spending his first night at Peak County Hospital.

When they arrived, Eric was propped up in bed, sipping juice through a straw and flipping television channels with the remote control.

"Good thing you didn't break your arm instead of your leg," Al teased. "What would you do if your channel-flipper arm was in a cast?"

"That would be rough," Eric admitted with a laugh.

"How are you doing?" Jon took a seat next to the bed.

"Much better," said Eric. "The night was a little

rough, but they gave me some pain medication."

"Did you eat any of your breakfast?" asked Bonnie. Jon knew his mom always worried about what he and Eric were eating, had eaten, or were planning to eat in the future!

"It's pretty nasty stuff." Eric lifted the cover off a bowl of gray, lumpy oatmeal. "And the toast was stone cold. What I really feel like is a breakfast burrito with lots of hot sauce!"

"You must be feeling better, then," said Al.

"Well, I don't think I ate much yesterday."

"Except for the granola bar I gave you," Jon reminded him.

"That's right! That tasted pretty darn good at the time."

Al smiled at Jon. "You did absolutely the right thing to take your backpack and survival gear, Jon. It's what I've tried to drill into both of you since you were old enough to play outside."

"It's so true!" said Bonnie. "You never know when you'll need emergency gear in the Rocky Mountains."

"Don't worry," Eric assured them. "I've learned my lesson!"

"Good," said Bonnie. "And now we all know how to construct an emergency sled. Thanks to Jon!"

"That's right," agreed Eric. "Hey, Jon-O. Did I ever say thanks for saving my life?"

Jon laughed. "Yep, you did. But you can tell me again."

"Thanks for saving my life, little brother. You were awesome! I feel pretty bad for all the times I've teased you about your inventions."

Al cleared his throat and looked at Eric. "That's something we all need to change. We need to give Jon the same kind of support for being an inventor that we've given you for skiing. Agreed?"

"Agreed!" said Eric. "Besides, I think one of Jon's inventions might make us all rich some-day."

"And you might make it to the Olympics some-day," added Jon.

"Maybe." Eric took a long pause. "But I have a

long road ahead if I'm going to make a comeback after this injury."

"Lots and lots of athletes come back after an injury," said Bonnie. "You'll just have to work hard with the physical therapist and take things a day at a time."

Eric nodded and looked down at the cast that reached his knee. "I learned a hard lesson." His voice was low and sad. "This never would have happened if I'd stayed with Jon and not tried to show off. I think I'm being reminded that showing off isn't the most important thing in the world."

"When will they let you go home?" asked Jon.

"Tomorrow. They just want to make sure I stay long enough to enjoy a few more of their delicious meals!"

Just then there was a knock at the door.

"Come in!" Eric hollered.

In burst Ronny and Drake, carrying take-out bags from a fast-food restaurant.

"Breakfast burritos!" shouted Ronny.

"With hot sauce!" Drake added.

Eric moaned with pleasure. "Ah, man! You guys read my mind."

"Hey, kid," Ronny said to Jon. "I heard you saved the day."

"Yeah," said Drake, "everybody's talking about you and your dog."

"They are?" Jon was stunned. "How do people know about it?"

"Because they read it in the papers," Drake said. He pulled a rolled-up newspaper out of his pocket and snapped it open with a flourish. "Right here on page one of the *Peak Daily*."

"You're kidding?" Jon couldn't believe it. "I made the paper?"

"Not once but twice!" Ronny said. "Not even your big brother, Mr. Hot Dog Skier, has made the paper *twice* in one day."

"Twice?" Jon said. "I don't understand."

"May I see that?" Al asked.

Drake handed the paper to Al, who read out loud.

" 'YOUNGER BROTHER SAVES
INJURED SKIER

'With the help of his loyal dog, Mogul, ten-year-old Jon Ziller rescued his older brother, Eric, who was injured while skiing the backcountry west of their home in the Peak Valley.

'After the boys became separated late Sunday afternoon, champion skier Eric Ziller broke his ankle in an unexpected fall near Fig Creek. Their Bernese Mountain Dog led Jon to his brother, and the younger boy used two sets of skis and poles to fashion a makeshift sled. The dog was harnessed to the sled, and pulled Eric in foot-deep snow to safety.

'Paramedics credit the younger Ziller for saving his brother from a potentially dangerous situation. "It was extremely stormy and cold when the incident happened," said paramedic Jane Lehman. "Eric was lucky not to have suffered frostbite or hypothermia. Jon Ziller handled the whole thing with intelligence and calm."

'Eric Ziller, who is recovering in the hospital, said he is very grateful to both his dog and his brother. "Jon," he said, "is the best brother a guy could ever have. He's my hero." ' "

Everyone clapped and whistled when Al finished reading. Jon was overwhelmed to have all those nice things said about him — especially by Eric.

"When did they interview you?" Bonnie asked.

"Last night," Eric said, smiling. "I was kind of out of it, but I wanted them to have my statement."

"Thanks," Jon said, trying not to blush in front of Drake and Ronny.

"And that's not all," Al said. "Listen to this."

But just then, there was a knock at the door.

"Come in!" Eric called.

The door was pushed open and Rosie and Polly appeared. Polly held a huge bunch of flowers wrapped in paper.

"Hey, you didn't have to bring me flowers!" Eric said.

"I didn't," Polly replied.

"They're for Jon," Rosie said with a huge grin. "For being a hero." She handed the flowers to Jon and patted him on the back. "Way to go, Jon. You scored a big one for inventors everywhere!"

"Wow. Thanks," Jon said. "That's really nice."

"How's your leg?" Polly asked Eric.

"Well, I won't be skiing or dancing anytime soon."

"But you can still lift weights," Ronny added.

"Yeah," said Drake. "We're going to make sure you stay in shape!"

Jon and Rosie rolled their eyes at each other.

"Oh!" said Rosie. "I almost forgot! More good news!"

"That's what I was trying to tell him," said Al, pointing to the paper.

"What?" Jon asked.

"Here." Al handed the paper to Rosie. "I think you should be the one to read this to Jon."

Rosie took the paper, cleared her throat, and read the headline out loud.

" 'ROSIE JOHNSON AND JON ZILLER
TAKE FIRST PLACE AT
INVENTION CONVENTION' "

"You're kidding!" Jon shouted.

"Says right there," Al said.

Jon jumped up and down with excitement. "Yes!" he shouted. "Yes!"

"Read it!" urged Bonnie.

"Well," said Rosie, "it shows a picture of Jon and me tossing water at Mogul. And it says:

" 'The judges for the annual Invention Convention at Peak Elementary School have announced the winners for this year's competition.

ROSIE JOHNSON
AND
JON ZILLER
TAKE FIRST
PLACE AT
INVENTION
CONVEN

'Taking first place is the fourth-grade team of Rosie Johnson and Jon Ziller, with their *"Wet Pet Splat Mat,"* which cleans and dries the family dog after a romp outdoors.' "

"Congratulations!" said Eric. "Way to go!"

"Then," said Rosie, "the article goes on to name the other winners."

"That is wonderful news, Jon!" Bonnie stood up to hug her son. Then she gave Rosie a hug, too. "Congratulations, Rosie!"

"Yeah," said Ronny. "Good job, Einsteins."

Just then a nurse came in with a tray. "It's time for Eric to have some medication. Can you all excuse us for a moment?"

The crowd filed out of the room and into the long hospital corridor.

Jon leaned against the wall, his head swimming with all the excitement. He still couldn't actually believe that he'd made the headlines and won first prize, all in one day!

Though he was having a great time, Jon

couldn't wait for things to return to normal. It seemed like a long time since he'd just hung out with Rosie or tossed a ball to Mogul.

"Shall we take you two back to school?" Bonnie asked.

Jon nodded his head. "Want to, Rosie?"

"Sure. Mrs. Hart told me they want us to pose for a picture to put on the wall at school."

Al handed Jon the newspaper. "Will they have an awards ceremony?"

"They usually do," Jon said. "And guess what? First-place winners get a trophy! It'll be my first one!"

"Mine, too!" said Rosie.

"Well, I want to be in the front row when that happens," Al said. "I'm really proud of you."

"Thanks! And now I need everyone to stop being proud of me. I don't think I can take much more!"

Bonnie poked her head in Eric's door to tell him they would be back soon, then they left the hospital and stepped outside into the bright winter sunshine.

"Let's go," Al said to Jon and Rosie.

"Okay. And Mom . . . ?"

"What?" Bonnie asked.

"Don't forget to fix Mogul those pancakes when you get home. And tell him I'll see him after school!"

On the way to school, Jon told Rosie about his idea for a new invention: dog food flavored with maple syrup, in the shape of tiny pancakes.

"No way!" Rosie replied. "This time we're doing an invention for cats."

"Dogs!" said Jon.

"Cats!"

Rosie laughed her famous laugh, which made Jon laugh, too.

Being a hero was great, but laughing with your best friend was even better!

And going home to the most incredible dog in the whole world was best of all.

Facts About
Bernese Mountain Dogs

1. Bernese Mountain Dogs are most often called Berners.
2. The Berner is one of four types of Swiss mountain dogs, which many believe are descendants of the Tibetan mastiff.
3. Berners are nicknamed "bear cubs" because of their size and coat.
4. They were first recognized as a breed in 1892.
5. They are the national dog of Switzerland. They were originally used in Switzerland to pull farm carts, and have also been used to herd cattle.

6. Because of their thick coats, they are well suited to cold climates.

7. They are most happy in rural environments with plenty of space to run and play.

8. They are loyal to family members, protective, and have a big desire to please.

9. They are nurturing, very communicative, and make wonderful family dogs.

10. An adult Berner can weigh from 75 to 110 pounds. They can reach a height of 23 to $27\frac{1}{2}$ inches.

11. They are black with tan markings and very solidly built. They have dark brown eyes and a bushy tail that curls at the end.

12. Berners are prone to some genetic health problems and have a shorter-than-average life span — on average eight years.

These facts were compiled from the following sources:

1. *The Reader's Digest Illustrated Book of Dogs,*

rev. 2nd ed. Pleasantville, NY: The Reader's
Digest Association, Inc., 1983.
2. Morn, September B. "Swiss Sentinel." *Dog
Fancy Magazine*, Volume 29, Number 2. (February 1998)

About the Author

Growing up in Denver, Colorado, Coleen Hubbard liked to write and put on plays in her backyard. As an adult, she still writes plays. She also now writes for children and young adults. Among her works are four books in the Treasured Horses series, which sparked her interest in writing fun books about animals and kids.

Coleen and her husband have three dog-crazy young daughters, plus Maggie the Magnificent, a sweet-natured mixed breed who inspired Coleen to learn all about the various breeds of dogs featured in the Dog Tales series.